13 3/13
6/15
L7x 11/17
29 5/19

Professor Tuesday's AWESOME ADVENTURES IN HISTORY

Book Two:
Migrating to Michigan

JEFFERY L. SCHATZER

mitten press

All inquiries should be addressed to:
Mitten Press
An imprint of Ann Arbor Media Group LLC
2500 S. State Street
Ann Arbor, MI 48104

Printed and bound at Edwards Brothers, Inc., Ann Arbor,
Michigan

10   9   8   7   6   5   4   3   2   1

Library of Congress Cataloging Data on File.

ISBN: 978-1-58726-604-1

Contents

No School

Outside Arrowhead School—Today

I don't know why I'm always the one who gets caught in the middle of things. Rachel is angry with Owen, and she won't talk to him. Owen is mad at Rachel, and he won't talk to her. So, I have to waste my whole day playing monkey-in-the-middle between the two of them. If Miss Pepper hadn't asked me to come along, I'd be playing with the rest of my friends.

"R-r-r-r! I am mad!" Rachel said. "Everybody else at Arrowhead School has the day off for the teachers' conference. But, not me! Why do I have to work with Owen on a special report for Miss Pepper?"

"Jesse," Owen said to me, "tell Rachel to hurry up. The sooner we get this over, the sooner we can enjoy our time off from school like everybody else."

I stopped and looked at Rachel. "Owen wants me to ask you to hurry up, please."

"I heard what he said. You can tell Owen that I'm coming. You can also tell him to stop bugging me." Rachel stopped talking and crossed her arms, "For another matter, he knew we were going to visit Professor Tuesday today. He could have at least worn some decent clothes."

"First off," Owen answered as he turned to me, "SHE is as much to blame as I am. We both got in trouble because we argue all the time. Besides, what's wrong with my clothes?"

"Look at him," Rachel said. "He's got on those baggy shorts and a messy T-shirt with a dog on it that says 'Bad to the Bone.' His glasses are broken, and there's tape on them. He's got his stupid ball cap on backwards and his high-tops are untied ... again."

I stomped my foot. "Hold it right now. Both of you need to calm down."

Owen and Rachel just stared at me. Nobody was happy, including me. It was a beautiful day. The sun was shining and birds chirped loudly. Other kids were laughing and playing outside in the warm sunshine. But, Owen and Rachel have an assignment to do ... and I'm stuck here in the middle between the two of them.

Suddenly, Owen's eyes got really big and his mouth opened wide. "AH-H-H-CHOO!" he sneezed into his elbow. "There must be a lot of pollen in the air."

6

"It's really good that you sneezed into your elbow," I said. "Miss Pepper says that's the best way to stop germs from spreading."

"He's always sneezing," Rachel said. "That's just one more thing that bugs me about him."

"She's always bratty," Owen said to me. "That's just one more thing that bugs me about her."

I crossed my arms and stared at both of my friends. "Look, if you two don't stop sniping at each other, I'm going home to enjoy my day off school. Will you at least try to be a little more kind to each other … at least for today?"

Owen and Rachel stopped for a moment. "Okay, I'll try," Owen said. Rachel just shook her head yes.

After walking the ten long blocks from our school to the university, we arrived at the building where the professor worked. We climbed the big stone steps to the entrance. Once we got there, it took all of Owen's might to open the large wooden door. Since it was Tuesday, we hoped that Professor Tuesday would be in his office.

As the door opened, I thought about the first time I ever saw Professor Tuesday. My class was on a field trip to meet him and learn about Chief Pontiac's war. Some kids in my class laughed at him, because he was so different. The professor has a long, bushy beard. His hair is mostly white and uncombed. A wide bald spot crowns the top of his head. His thick glasses generally hang low on his nose, and his eyes seem to always be moving back and forth.

Professor Tuesday looks kind of funny in his big glasses, doctor's coat, and bow tie. While he is very smart and very nice, he is a bit strange. The professor loves Tuesdays and does most things in twos. To top it all off, he invented a machine that can take people back in time, but it only works on Tuesdays, and it only goes back to Tuesdays in history.

As we spent time with him the day of our field trip, the class grew to like Professor Tuesday. I was looking forward to seeing him again, myself. I shivered as I stepped through the door of the university building. It was warm outside, but the inside of the big stone building was cool. Once inside, Rachel stepped up to a sign that was on the wall by the door.

"What is she looking at?" Owen asked.

I shrugged my shoulders. "I don't know."

"I'm looking at the building directory," she said. "Most buildings have the names of people or businesses posted on the wall. It's called a directory. The names of people who work in buildings like this are usually in alphabetical order."

Owen read aloud down the list of names on the chart. "Professor Adams, Professor Dowler, Professor Samson ... there he is ... Professor Tuesday 2C."

"That means the professor's office is on the second floor in room C," said Rachel.

"Duh, really?" Owen said smartly. Then he looked at me. "Sorry, I'll try to be a little nicer."

"C'mon, let's find him," Rachel said as we all headed up the wide stairs. She stopped on the steps and turned to Owen. "Did you bring your journal?

Miss Pepper said we were supposed to keep journals for the report."

"Of course I brought my journal," Owen replied as he slapped his journal against the wall. "Do you have yours?"

Rachel pulled her journal out of her backpack and gave Owen a funny look.

Tuesday Again
University Building—Today

We found the office in the middle of the building. Professor Tuesday's name was lettered on
the cloudy glass at the top of the closed door. There
weren't any lights on in the room. I worried that the
professor might not be in his office.

Owen knocked lightly at the door. There was
no answer. We waited several minutes, and then he
knocked again.

"Knock harder," Rachel said.

This time, Owen made a fist and pounded on
the door. The glass rattled and the old wooden door
creaked open a little bit. Owen looked at me and
shrugged his shoulders. Without saying a word, we
pushed the door slowly. The hinges on the heavy
door groaned as it swung open. When we poked our
heads inside, we couldn't see anybody.

The shades were drawn over the windows and all the lights were off. The office was so dark it took time for our eyes to adjust. Papers and books were stacked in high piles everywhere. The office was quiet and still.

We were about to turn around and leave when Owen whispered, "Look!" He pointed to the far side of the room. Two tiny lights moved back and forth steadily. We watched the lights as the three of us quietly stepped into the dark room.

"This is creepy," I whispered. "Turn on the lights."

Rachel peeked around the corner of the professor's desk as Owen went to turn on the light switch. Just before the lights came on, I saw him. The two tiny lights were on his glasses. He was reading a book in the dark.

When Owen flipped on the lights, the professor jumped and screamed. When Professor Tuesday screamed, Rachel, Owen, and I screamed.

The professor jumped up from his chair and hopped up on top of his desk. He held his chest with one hand and his head with the other. Then he hopped from one foot to the other. Once the screaming stopped, he started laughing. Then, Owen, Rachel, and I started laughing, too. It was quite a funny sight.

"That was a good scare," said Professor Tuesday. He smiled as he carefully climbed down from his desk and turned off the lights that were on his glasses. "I like a good scare now and then. It gets the old heart pumping!"

The professor straightened himself and looked at the three of us. "Now, to what do I owe the pleasure of this visit?"

Rachel looked at Owen, he looked at me, and we all shrugged. None of us could figure out what the professor meant.

The professor looked confused for a moment. Then he realized that we didn't understand his question. "Why are you here?"

"Oh," I answered, "my name is Jesse, and these are my friends Rachel and Owen. We are all in Miss Pepper's class at Arrowhead School."

"Oh, I remember your class," the professor said. "Your school came to the university on a field trip to learn about Chief Pontiac."

"That's right," I said. "Now, Owen and Rachel need your help with something."

Professor Tuesday blinked twice and looked right at me. "Owen and Rachel need my help, but what about you?"

Owen shuffled his feet and looked down at the floor as he spoke. "It's like this, Professor. Rachel and I got in trouble at school. It seems like we're always arguing about this and that. So, Miss Pepper gave us an assignment to work on together over the school break."

"Ah-h-h," the professor said as he stroked his long, white beard, "Jesse is here to be the peacemaker between you two. So, what is this special assignment?"

"We have to do a report on the immigrants who settled in Michigan," Owen answered.

The professor's eyes got wide with excitement. "What a great assignment!" he shouted. "I've been studying immigrants and immigration for years. In fact, I was just reading a book on the Finns in Michigan. It's very interesting."

"Professor, my family came to Michigan from Finland," Owen said proudly. "Can we go back in time to visit my relatives with your Tuesday Teleporter?"

"Perhaps," the professor replied. "I've got a few things I need to finish before I can help you with your research. While I attend to these matters, you can go get my nephew. He's in the library on the main floor of this building. Bring him back here, and we'll begin our research."

"Your nephew?" I asked.

"Yes," said the professor. "His name is Mister Adams. He is staying with me while my sister is on vacation. I'm sure he'd enjoy coming along with us."

Searching for Mister Adams
University Building—Today

The professor turned and started shuffling some papers as Owen, Rachel, and I left to search for Mister Adams. We went down the stairs and took another look at the building directory. There it was—the library was located in room 1A on the first floor of the building.

"Do you think we should have asked Professor Tuesday what Mister Adams looks like?" I asked.

"Nah," Owen answered as he wiped his nose on his sleeve. "There aren't many people in this building. I'm sure we'll be able to find him without any trouble."

As we walked down the hallway toward the library, Rachel's shoes made a clopping sound on the shiny black floor. Owen's sneakers made a squishy sound with each step he took. The sounds their shoes made echoed through the empty hallway. Before long, we were standing in front of the library. We pushed the door open and stepped inside.

The library was quiet and musty smelling. Our library at Arrowhead School has a media specialist who helps us with finding books, computer searches, and stuff. There wasn't a media specialist in this library, just rows and rows of high bookshelves and lots and lots of books.

Owen, Rachel, and I walked down the rows of bookshelves. Though there were tons of books, the library looked like it was empty of people. We searched row after row without seeing anyone. When we got to the very last row of shelves, we were surprised by what we saw. A little boy was sitting on top of a big book, scribbling on a piece of paper with a pencil. He looked to be about the same age as my little brother—maybe four years old. The boy had freckles and thick glasses. Little sprigs of hair stuck out all over his head.

"Hi," Owen said. "Have you seen Mister Adams around here anywhere?"

He didn't say a word. Instead, he stood up, looked at us, made some funny movements with his hands, and turned a page in the book. Then he sat back down again.

"Say," Owen said, "do you think he's Mister Adams?"

"No," Rachel said. "That can't be Mister Adams. He's just a little kid."

"Mister Adams must have left the library," I said to Owen. "Why don't we look through the rest of the building? Who knows, maybe he went back to the professor's office."

Owen and Rachel agreed and we left the library to search the building. The old building was almost completely empty. We only found one other person. A student was taking a test in one of the offices. She was definitely not Mister Adams.

We kept looking, searching every floor and every office. We didn't find the professor's nephew anywhere. We were getting worried so we went back to Professor Tuesday's office. We found the professor humming to himself as he fiddled with his laptop. When the professor noticed the three of us standing there, a curious look crossed his face.

"I thought you were going to get Mister Adams," the professor said.

"We looked through the library," I said. "In fact, we looked all through the building. We couldn't find him anywhere."

"What?" said the professor. "Oh my goodness, we've got to find him and find him now! There's no way I can go anywhere until we find him."

"But we've got a report that's due next Monday," Rachel said.

The professor stopped and turned to Rachel. "Mister Adams is my first responsibility. I'm sorry, but his safety is more important than your report. If we all work together to find him, we can begin your research. But we have to find him first."

We followed the professor as he raced out the door and down the hallway. All the while, the professor called out for his nephew. "Mister Adams! Mister Adams! Come here, you rascal."

The professor climbed up on the hand railing and slid down the staircase all the way to the first floor of the building. He jumped off the railing when he got to the bottom and took off down the hallway toward the library. "We must find him or my sister will be very angry with me," the professor said. "Mister Adams has a bad habit of wandering off."

When the professor entered the library, Owen called out to him. "Professor, we already looked in the library. Nobody's in there but a ..."

Just then we heard the professor shout with joy. "There you are, Mister Adams. I thought you were lost." The professor came out of the library with the little boy in his arms.

"That's Mister Adams?" Owen said. "We thought that Mister Adams would be a grown person."

"Heavens, no," said the professor. "This is my nephew, Mister Adams."

"If you don't mind me asking, Professor," I said, "how did a little kid get a name like 'Mister Adams'?"

The professor blinked twice and scratched his bald head. "You see, my sister wanted her son to have an important sounding name. She likes history, too. And, her favorite president of the United States was John Adams. Abigail Adams, the wife of President Adams, often referred to him as 'Mr. Adams.' That's how he got his name. Don't you think that's an important sounding name?"

17

"Strange," said Owen as he took off his ball cap and shook his head back and forth. "But I guess that makes sense, kind of."

"Maybe so," said the professor, "but when people meet Mister Adams they never forget him. Even though he's just a small child, he can read and write very well. He was in the library helping me on a project. Mister Adams is very smart, but there's one thing you should know about him. He doesn't like to talk."

"You said that we had to take Mister Adams with us on our adventure today," Rachel noted. "What are we going to do with a little kid tagging along?"

The professor looked at the three of us. "All of you can help me watch him. He is quite adventurous, so we'll have to keep a close eye on him."

Rachel rolled her eyes as the professor started back toward his office with Mister Adams. I happen to know that Rachel doesn't like babysitting ... not even for her own little brother. Now, we have to watch Mister Adams AND my friends have to do an extra assignment.

This was starting to look like one crummy school break.

Digging into Immigrant History
The Professor's Office—Today

When we got back to the professor's office, he gave Mister Adams a thick, heavy Michigan history book to read. Then he took a seat behind his desk and folded his hands and twiddled his thumbs as he spoke. "Mister Adams," the professor said, "I want you to read about early Michigan history. That should keep you occupied and out of trouble for a while."

Then, the professor turned to Rachel and Owen. "Now," he said, "you mentioned that you have to do a report on people who have immigrated to Michigan. Is that correct?"

"Yup," Owen said. "Can we take your Tuesday Teleporter back in time to visit immigrants?"

The professor stroked his long white beard while he thought. "I suppose we can. But, what immigrant groups would you like to visit?"

"All of them," Rachel said. "Miss Pepper wants us to do a report on the immigrants who have come to Michigan, so we should visit all of them."

"That won't be possible, my friends," the professor began. "Many, many different immigrants have come to Michigan. It has been that way since the first Europeans came here in the 1600s. We couldn't possibly visit them all in one Tuesday. In fact, we probably couldn't visit them all in a month of Tuesdays."

"Well," Rachel said, "when we visited you with our class, we learned about the Native Americans, the French, and the British. Maybe we could visit all the other immigrants."

"That is still too many groups to visit," he said. The professor cleaned his glasses with his coat sleeves, then snapped his fingers twice before continuing. "Immigrants from foreign nations are still settling in Michigan. One of my students came here from the Sudan ten years ago. He will be coming to my office later today if you want to talk to him."

"Okay," Rachel said, "that would be fine. But what do you think we should do about the rest of our report? Shouldn't we get information about other immigrant groups?"

"I've got an idea," said the professor. "Do you know where your families originally came from?"

Rachel thought for a moment. "My dad's family is German. My grandma lives in Frankenmuth. As for my mother, her parents are Dutch and Irish."

Owen spoke up, "My mom's Finnish, and my dad is Polish. Can we visit the early Finns and Poles?"

"We'll do our best," said the professor. "We need to do a little research first. I'll look for information about early settlements of Germans and Dutch in Michigan." The professor bent down low and spoke to Mister Adams. "While you are reading about early Michigan, please look for information on Finnish and Polish immigrants."

Mister Adams took a paper and pencil and wrote down some notes. Then he dug into the history book the professor had given him. Professor Tuesday opened a different history book that was on the corner of his desk. Rachel decided to help the professor. Owen and I went to work with Mister Adams.

I was starting to feel better about being here with my friends. They hadn't argued for almost a whole half hour.

Owen and I followed Mister Adams to the table at the far side of the professor's office. The professor's nephew pulled some books from a shelf, and we started doing our own research.

Professor Tuesday put on his reading glasses and paged through the index of his book. "Hm-m-m, let's see," he said aloud. "It says here that Germans immigrated to the United States as far back as the 1800s. Many came here for work. However, some also came to establish missionary settlements."

The professor read to himself for a while. Then he noted: "Many Germans in Michigan were experienced miners. Miners tended to settle in the Keweenaw Peninsula where they found work in the copper mines. Several immigrants from Germany were farmers who established communities near

Ann Arbor and other areas of Michigan, including in the Saginaw Valley where Rachel's grandmother lives."

Suddenly, Mister Adams jumped up on his seat and made some strange motions with his hands. Owen and I thought he was freaking out. We didn't know what was going on, so we ran over to the professor for help.

"Professor," Owen said excitedly, "Mister Adams is acting weird."

"Weird, like how?" asked the professor.

"Well," Owen said as he shuffled his feet, "it's kind of hard to explain. He made the letter c with his right hand and put it by his throat and moved it down to his chest."

"Do you think he's using sign language?" Rachel asked.

"He is," the professor noted. "Mister Adams is trying to tell you that he is hungry."

"Mister Adams doesn't like to talk, so he uses sign language?" Rachel asked.

"He sure does," the professor said, "and he's pretty good at it. Sometimes, he signs so fast I can't even understand him."

Without a word, Professor Tuesday left his office and headed down the hallway. After a few minutes, he returned with a tray of fruit and cheese. He cut and peeled an apple for Mister Adams. Then he gave him a piece of cheese.

Mister Adams put his hands to his lips, then moved it outward. "That's the sign for 'thank you,'" Owen said.

"Very good," said the professor. "I think that we'll all get along nicely."

"Yah, right," Rachel stared at Owen.

After he gave Mister Adams his snack, the professor turned to Rachel, Owen, and me. "Help yourself."

Rachel and I both took an orange and Owen had a pear. After our snack, we went back to work.

"Well," the professor said to me with a smile, "I think we should visit Frankenmuth in the summer of 1846. We've got everything we need to make the trip. Let's see how your friends and Mister Adams are doing with their research."

"Owen isn't MY friend," Rachel said. "We argue all the time. That's why Miss Pepper told us to do this assignment together over the school break."

"I see," said Professor Tuesday, "it is very interesting that Miss Pepper gave you this assignment."

"What do you mean?" Owen asked.

The professor chuckled. "Many different people have come to settle the state of Michigan. Sometimes they struggled to get along with each other, just like you and Rachel. But, when they started working together, they made our state a very special place. Maybe this assignment is Miss Pepper's way of helping you get along and learn some history all at the same time."

"I don't see that happening in my lifetime," I said with a snicker.

The professor just laughed and shook his head.

Mister Adams had three pages of notes about the early Finns in Michigan. Owen was scanning a book about Finnish immigrants to the state.

"This is pretty cool," Owen said. "Many Finns moved to the Upper Peninsula to work in the copper mines. Some also worked as lumberjacks during the lumbering era. Do you think we can visit some Finns, Professor?"

"I believe so," said the professor, "but I'd like to ask for Mister Adams's thoughts."

Mister Adams turned his head toward us and smiled. Then his hand went into a flurry of motion. He was using the sign language alphabet to spell out his ideas.

"Whoa," said the professor as he chuckled aloud, "you're signing too fast. Slow down a bit."

Mister Adams gave the professor a funny look, then started signing all over again. As his hands moved through the air, the professor wrote down each letter.

E_R_I_E C_A_N_A_L

"What a great idea, Mister Adams," said the professor. "Before we visit any immigrant settlements in Michigan, we should visit the construction of the Erie Canal. I'm even thinking we should make one more stop before we visit the immigrants."

"What does a canal have to do with immigration?" Owen asked.

"We shall see," said the professor, "we shall see."

Immigrant's Path
The Erie Canal near Buffalo, New York—June 1826

Professor Tuesday hooked up the teleporter with its shiny globe to his laptop and typed in some information on the keyboard. Then, he snapped his fingers twice.

"Turn off the lights," the professor said.

Owen ran over to the wall and flipped the switch. In the darkened room we could see the professor raise two fingers in the air. "I've made some changes to my teleporter," he said. "Watch this."

Professor Tuesday came down on the enter key on his laptop. The Tuesday Teleporter lit up like a pinball machine and made strange zapping sounds. Different colored lights slowly circled the room. Then they started moving faster and faster. The sounds got louder and louder.

"AH-H-H-H-CHOO," Owen sneezed into his elbow. "I think I'm allergic to your teleporter, Professor."

"Ah, yes," said the professor, "now I remember you, Owen. You almost got us in trouble with your sneezing when we visited a Native American village in Ohio."

POW! ZING! went the machine. Then a green cloud appeared in the middle of the professor's office.

"Did it break?" Rachel asked. "I don't remember that noise. And, the teleporter I remember looked more like a green gob than a cloud."

"Everything's fine," said the professor. "Those are the improvements I made. I figured out a way to make the teleporter appear in the form of a cloud rather than a gob of jelly. People didn't like walking through jelly. They like the cloud much better."

After he made a few more keystrokes on his laptop, the professor turned to us. "Please watch Mister Adams for a moment while I make sure everything is perfectly safe."

The professor turned and walked into the green cloud. Mister Adams pointed his fingers in the air, then made a quick movement forward.

"Oh," I said, "Mister Adams wants to go. That's what that sign means."

Mister Adams shook his head excitedly.

"Yes," I said to him, "we'll all go with the professor when he returns."

Then Mister Adams nodded his head and went back to his history book. Maybe it wouldn't be too bad watching Mister Adams for the professor. Besides, sign language can be fun.

The professor walked out of the green cloud after a few moments. "It's a lovely day in 1826," said the professor. "Let's go."

We all held hands. Professor Tuesday was in the lead. Then it was me, Rachel, Owen, and Mister Adams.

Once inside the cloud, we started tumbling end-over-end. Lights flashed by us and Owen sneezed again. Mister Adams tried to let go of Owen's hand, but Owen held on tightly.

We landed softly in the middle of a thick forest. There were trees, bushes, and grass for as far as we could see. "I thought we were going to see the Erie Canal?" I asked.

The professor turned to me. "Now is the time for watching and taking notes. There will be time for asking questions later."

The professor reached into his white coat and pulled out a compass. Then he started walking south. The forest was so thick that it was hard to walk. We stepped around fallen trees and through thickets of prickly bushes.

As we walked, Owen stepped in a muddy creek bed. When he tried to get his foot out, he got stuck. We all had to wait patiently while he pulled his shoe from the mud and put it back on his foot. From then on, his shoe made squishy sounds with every step.

"Owen," Rachel said, "can't you do anything right?"

"It's not my fault," he answered. "I didn't mean to get my foot stuck."

Mister Adams held up his finger to his lips.

"Mister Adams is right," said the professor. "We should be quiet."

When we came to the top of a high hill, the professor stopped and pointed down to the valley below. There it was, the Erie Canal. The canal was a long and narrow strip of water. It was so long we couldn't see either end of it. Owen and Rachel started scribbling in their journals. They wanted to record everything they were seeing.

The professor was right, it was a beautiful day. There wasn't a cloud in the sky. The water in the canal sparkled in the sunlight. All was quiet except for the sound coming from the small town on the other side of the Erie Canal.

Boats and barges were moving along the waterway in both directions. They were being pulled by teams of horses that walked along the banks. Just below us, a boat entered something that looked like a long box with stone sides. As we watched, the boat seemed to rise. Then the young man who was driving the horses snapped the reins. Next, the horses pulled the boat to another big box where it rose again and continued up the canal.

Professor Tuesday reached into his coat pocket and took out some binoculars. We all took turns looking at the waterway and the town below. Some boats were carrying people, others carried barrels and boxes.

"Look around carefully," said the professor. "There is much to see and learn here, but we can't stay long."

Off in the distance, a wagon made its way along a dirt road on the other side of the waterway. Clouds of dust were coming from its wheels as it bumped along. It looked like the wagon was heading for the town by the canal. When I looked through the binoculars, I could pick out the white steeple of a church, some stores, and a few homes along the hillside.

Even though there were only a few buildings down by the canal, the small town was a beehive of activity. Men were hauling carts toward the dock that ran alongside the bank. It also looked like some adults and children were waiting nearby.

Mister Adams Wanders
Near Buffalo, New York—June 1826

"This is a beautiful place," Owen said as he looked around.

"Indeed it is," answered the professor. "In the future, there will be homes, villages, and roads dotting this countryside. In 1826, it is very primitive.

We watched the canal and quietly listened to the sounds of nature for several minutes.

"It's time to go back now," said the professor. "Where's Mister Adams?" The professor looked upset. "Now, where is that pesky nephew of mine?"

Owen swallowed with a loud gulp. "It's not my fault. He was here just a minute ago."

"It's never your fault," Rachel said. "Can't you do anything right?"

"I'm sorry," said Owen, "but you don't have to yell at me every time I make a mistake. Nobody's perfect, you know."

"Back off, Rachel," I said, "Owen said he was sorry. Besides, we need to work together to find Mister Adams."

"He's got to be somewhere nearby, he hasn't been gone all that long," the professor said. We started searching for him. "We should all be careful not to get lost while we're looking for Mister Adams."

We walked in a big circle looking for the professor's nephew. The brush was thick, making it hard to see very far. We were all getting a little scared.

As we walked, we called out Mister Adams's name, but there was no answer. I was hoping that he would speak up when he was called. If he was in trouble and using sign language, we wouldn't know. Owen got all scratched up as he made his way through some picky bushes.

Rachel was upset. This trip wasn't turning out the way she planned. Mister Adams was nowhere to be found. And, she was afraid that the professor's nephew might just ruin her chances of getting a good grade on her report.

We completed a big circle without finding Mister Adams. It was easy to see that the professor was getting worried. When we returned to the place where we started, the professor looked up as he scratched his bald head. "Oh, there he is," the professor said, with relief, as he pointed to a nearby tree. "Thank goodness we found you. Now, get down here this minute."

Mister Adams was sitting on a branch in the tree. The professor's nephew made a sign that I didn't understand. It was like an 'okay' sign that he made by his face. Then he moved it toward the back of his head and pointed to the horizon. Then he spelled out a word.

"What is he saying, Professor?" Rachel asked.

"Mister Adams sees a group of Native Americans," said the professor. "It looks like they are coming this way."

"What tribe are they from?" I asked.

"Mister Adams says he doesn't know for sure," said the professor, "but he thinks they may be a hunting party from a nearby Seneca tribe."

"Are we in danger?" I asked.

Professor Tuesday shook his head. "I don't think we are in any danger, but I want to take you somewhere else. We need to be getting back to my office."

Mister Adams climbed down from the tree. When he got to the lowest branch, he swung back and forth a few times before jumping to the ground.

The professor took a long look at his compass. Then we started back through the deep woods to the place we started this adventure. Owen's one shoe squished with every step he took. When we got back to the creek he had stepped in, he was careful to jump over it this time.

I could tell that the professor wasn't happy with his nephew. I hoped he would let Owen and Rachel finish their research, but I wasn't sure.

Journey to the Melting Pot of Michigan
Detroit—July 1837

O nce we stepped through the green cloud and back into Professor Tuesday's office, the professor turned to his nephew. "Mister Adams, you gave us quite a scare back there. What if you had wandered off and gotten lost? I want you to promise that you'll stay with us, or I'll have to find a babysitter to stay here with you for the rest of the day."

I could tell that Rachel thought that getting a babysitter for the professor's nephew was a great idea. Mister Adams looked very sad. Slowly he raised his right hand to his chest and made the letter *s*, then his hand made a circle in front of his heart.

Rachel pointed at Mister Adams, "I think that sign means he's sorry."

"Very good, Rachel," said Professor Tuesday. "Is everyone ready to go on another adventure?"

"Sure," Owen said, "but aren't we going to talk about our trip to the Erie Canal?"

The professor nodded his head, "Yes, we'll talk about the Erie Canal when we get to Detroit."

"Are we going to Detroit, now?" Rachel asked. "My dad goes to Detroit on business. He even takes me with him sometimes. Maybe we can see a ball-game or go to the zoo."

The professor gave Rachel a knowing smile. "I don't think there will be a ballgame on our visit, but there's no doubt we'll see some animals."

Rachel clapped her hands and jumped up and down in excitement. "I love animals."

"I think everything is ready now," said the professor as he started up the teleporter for a second visit into history. "I'll just poke my head into the cloud to take a look around before we travel."

It looked funny when the professor stuck his head into the green cloud. With his head inside, he looked like a headless body that stood in front of us. After a moment he pulled it back. "Everything is just fine. Wait until you see this. You won't believe it."

We held hands once again, this time with Mister Adams between Owen and me. We didn't want him to wander off again. Even with all the loud noises the teleporter made, all of us could hear Owen sneeze once more as we traveled through time.

We came through the green cloud and landed on a grassy hill overlooking a frontier town at the edge of the water. "Welcome to Detroit," said the professor.

"This can't be Detroit," Rachel said. "Where are the tall buildings? Where are the expressways and all the cars? What about the airplanes and helicopters? This doesn't look anything like Detroit."

The professor let out a loud laugh. "My dear," he said, "this is Detroit as it was in 1837, long before they had cars, planes, professional sports teams, museums, and zoos."

"But you said that we'd see animals," Rachel pouted.

"We'll see lots of animals," the professor replied. "Just you wait and see." The professor sat down on the grassy hill and took off his shoes and socks.

"What are you doing, Professor?" I asked.

"Don't you just love the feeling of grass between your toes?" he asked.

"I sure do," said Owen as he pulled off his high-tops and socks. His one shoe and sock were still covered with mud. Soon all of us were lying back on the hill with grass between our toes. Big, billowy clouds hung in the blue sky above our heads. Owen saw one that looked like a dragon. Rachel found one that looked like a car, kind of.

Mister Adams started jumping up and down and pointing toward a cloud that was over the lake. He made his right hand in the shape of the letter *a* and covered it with his left hand. Then he moved his right thumb back and forth.

"What's he saying, Professor?" Owen asked.

The professor looked at Mister Adams and then at the clouds. "He's saying he sees a cloud that looks like a turtle."

We all had a good laugh. As we relaxed on the hillside, the professor started to ask us questions.

"So, why do you think Detroit is a busy town in 1837?" asked the professor.

"It is because the city is on water," Owen replied.

"I think it's because of the Erie Canal," said Rachel.

"Me, too," I said.

"All of you are correct," said the professor. "The Erie Canal was one of the main reasons Detroit became an important city in the 1800s. The canal made it much easier for people and supplies to travel from New York to the Midwest." The professor chewed on a piece of grass as he thought. "What did you write in your journals about the canal?"

Owen opened his journal and looked up at the professor. "I wrote down that it was one big ditch."

Even Rachel laughed at what he had written.

"Funny that you should call it a 'ditch'," said the professor. "When Governor Clinton of New York decided to build the Erie Canal, some politicians didn't like the idea. In fact, they often called the project 'Clinton's Ditch'."

"That is funny," I said.

"So, what did we learn on our trip to visit the Erie Canal?" asked the professor.

"For one thing," Rachel said smartly, "we learned that Owen didn't do a good job of watching Mister Adams."

"AH-H-H-CHOO!" Owen sneezed into his elbow. Then he looked down as he spoke, "I'm sorry, Professor. I should have been more careful."

"Well," said the professor, "you made a mistake, and I was scared that we might lose Mister Adams for a while. What is important is that we all learn from our mistakes. In fact, making mistakes is an important way we learn. Next time we will all be more careful."

Owen nodded his head in agreement. Mister Adams just smiled and shook his head yes.

"Exactly why is the canal so important to our study of immigrants?" Rachel asked.

The professor looked up at the sky as he spoke. "Traveling over land took much longer and it was more difficult than traveling through a waterway. Once the Erie Canal was built, immigrants had an easy and inexpensive route to Michigan. People poured into our state from all over the world. It was the Erie Canal that made it possible for so many new people to come to here."

Professor Tuesday raised one shoulder then the other. "The idea for the Erie Canal started in the late 1700s. Robert Fulton, himself, sent a letter to George Washington in 1797 to ask for his support for the canal."

"Robert Fulton," I asked, "wasn't he the guy who invented the steam engine or something like that?"

"Very good," said the professor. "Fulton was a famous inventor who came from Ireland. He also was very interested in a canal that would help to open up North America to new settlement and trade."

"Did I mention that I'm part Irish?" Rachel asked proudly.

"I believe you did," answered the professor.

Chilling on a Hillside
Detroit – July 1837

Professor Tuesday picked a leaf off of his coat before he continued. "A survey was done in 1816 that established the route of the Erie Canal. It was to run from the Hudson River, not far from what is now New York City, to Lake Erie near Buffalo, New York. Work started on the canal in 1817, and it was finished in 1825."

"Who did all the work?" Owen asked as he scratched his nose.

The professor smiled. "Thousands of immigrants helped to build it. British, Irish, and Germans provided much of the work. Keep in mind that, back in those days, they didn't have big construction equipment like front-end loaders, dump trucks, and bulldozers. The entire canal had to be dug by hand and with the help of horses and other work animals."

"So, how long was the canal?" Rachel asked.

"When it was first built, the Erie Canal was 363 miles long. That's about the same distance between Detroit, Michigan, and Louisville, Kentucky," said the professor. "It was also 40 feet wide and 4 feet deep."

"Holy cow," Owen said. "That's a long way and a lot of digging."

The professor looked at us without saying anything. Suddenly, Owen spoke up again. "I saw something else that was interesting. One boat went into a big rock box and it seemed to float up a bit."

"Excellent," said Professor Tuesday. "You saw a lock."

"A lock, like on my locker at school?" I asked.

"No, locks on a locker are different. Waterway locks were used by the canal's designers to lift boats up to the level of Lake Erie or down to the level of the Hudson River," said the professor. "You see, Lake Erie is about 560 feet higher than the Hudson River. So locks were built to lift or lower boats and barges as they traveled along the canal. If the boat is heading toward Lake Erie, it would enter a lock and water would be added to raise it up. When a boat was headed toward the Hudson River from Lake Erie, it would be lowered by the locks. As I recall, there were about 85 locks needed for the canal. In its day, the Erie Canal was thought to be a miracle of engineering. And it was."

The professor thought for a moment before speaking. "In those days, there were very few roads.

The entire countryside was like the thick woods where we first started out. So, to travel over land from New York City to Buffalo, New York, may have taken weeks. The Erie Canal allowed people and cargo to travel the same distance in about four days."

I nodded my head.

"Professor," Owen said, "I heard some kids shouting to the horses alongside the canal. What was that all about?"

"Good question," said the professor. "Teams of horses were used to pull boats and barges along a special pathway. The 'hoggees' who drove these teams of horses along the paths were just boys."

"Driving horses along the canal ... that sounds like a pretty cool job," Owen said. "I would have picked a different name for it, though."

"I should think so," Professor Tuesday agreed.

"So, did you take us to the Erie Canal to show us how immigrants built it?" I asked.

Mister Adams then made a circular motion with his hands in front of his body.

"That's right, Mister Adams," the professor noted. "I wanted everyone to see that one of the boats on the canal was carrying people. In fact, people in the small town on the other side of the canal looked like they were taking goods down to the canal. Did you also notice the people and families waiting on the dock? The Erie Canal opened up migration to the west, and it made it much easier to travel to states like Michigan. Much of the reason Michigan has such a diverse culture is due to the construction of the Erie Canal. It wouldn't be long before roads and railroads would crisscross the country, eliminating the need for the canal. But the canal served its purpose for many years."

A Walk through Frontier Detroit
Detroit—July 1837

Professor Tuesday put his shoes and socks back on, then stood up and stretched. "Let's all go for a walk in Detroit to see what it looked like in 1837."

The professor started off toward town when Owen shouted, "Hey, where's Mister Adams?"

"Oh, no, not again," Rachel said.

The professor looked upset, so we all started looking for his nephew. Fortunately, our search didn't take long. Mister Adams was fast asleep at the base of a tree on the grassy hill. Professor Tuesday gently woke him. As we headed toward town, Mister Adams used sign language to tell us about a dream he had. It was about a cat chasing a big dog.

Before long, we were standing near the waterfront. Sailing ships and a few steamships crowded the large docks. Workers were taking heavy loads of goods off the ships and carrying them to shore on wagons. As we watched, a loud steamship whistle blew as a boat approached the docks. Sailors tied the ship to big wooden posts and dropped a walkway from the boat to the dock. People milled around on the ship as they started to make their way toward land. Families gathered their children and led them across the walkway and toward us. Many of the travelers were carrying large sacks and luggage.

The professor stopped and turned toward us, "Detroit was a major port city in 1837. The people who immigrated to Michigan in those days usually came through this very spot. It was a busy city even then. I read that in 1837 about 200,000 people entered and left Detroit."

"Where did they go?" Rachel asked.

"Some of them moved into the state and formed many of the cities and towns we know in our time. Others moved on to the west to join their families as the country began to grow."

"How many people lived in Detroit in 1837?" Owen asked.

"Only about 10,000 lived in the city of Detroit itself," the professor said. "Wayne County, the county that Detroit is in, had over 23,000."

"There are a lot more today," Owen noted.

"Professor, do you think that those were immigrants coming off that steamship?" I asked.

"Many of them may be immigrants," said the professor. "Some could be traders or people traveling to the territorial capital. In the early 1800s,

Michigan was the most popular destination in the country for people who wanted to move west into the frontier."

Across the street from us, men were loading animal furs into crates and stacking them near the docks. Others were putting crates on wagons and loading them aboard a sailing ship. I made sure that I watched Mister Adams carefully as we continued to look around.

Professor Tuesday pointed toward the men working nearby. "The fur trade was big business in early Michigan," he said. "One of the most important businessmen in his day was John Jacob Astor. His fur business extended throughout the state and into nearby territories. Astor's main office was here in Detroit, and he had a business on Mackinac Island as well. However, he probably never visited the island himself. He sold off his entire business in 1834 because he was getting old and sick."

"So," Owen said, "there was a big business in Michigan that provided beaver furs. Did they use the furs to make coats?"

"Most of the furs were used to make hats," answered the professor, "but beaver hats went out of fashion in about 1850. The industry died off soon after John Jacob Astor sold his business."

The professor tapped me on the shoulder and pointed. "Let's go this way."

As we were about to cross the dirt road, what looked like a stagecoach came roaring toward us. Professor Tuesday held out his arms and pushed us all out of the way. Dust from the wheels churned up in clouds all around us. Rachel coughed. Owen sneezed. Mister Adams and I covered our eyes.

"Is that what I think it is?" I asked.

"If you think it's a stagecoach, you're right," answered the professor. "In 1834 a stagecoach line started between Detroit and St. Joseph, Michigan. Most of the passengers on this line would pick up a steamship in St. Joseph and travel westward. Then, in 1835, two stagecoaches a week traveled between Detroit and Fort Dearborn."

"I suppose that Fort Dearborn was in Dearborn, Michigan," Rachel said. "Isn't that where the Henry Ford Museum is?"

"Dearborn, Michigan, and Fort Dearborn are two very different places," the professor said with a smile. "In the 1800s, Fort Dearborn was what we call Chicago in our time. And, yes, the Henry Ford Museum and Greenfield Village are located in Dearborn, Michigan, but Henry Ford didn't start collecting items for his museum until the early 1900s."

When the road was clear, we crossed. The street was dirty and dusty. Owen sneezed over and over as we walked by large buildings that looked like warehouses. Boxes and barrels were being hauled in and out. People were everywhere as we walked down the street. Some pushed two-wheeled carts. Some were selling vegetables or blankets. Cows, pigs, horses, chickens, geese, and mules were being led along the road. It was very noisy. People along the streets talked in many different languages. It was also very smelly because of all the animals.

"Here are the animals you wanted to see, Rachel," the professor said with a smile.

Rachel held her nose in disgust. "It smells terrible here. And, these aren't the kinds of animals I wanted to see."

Owen and I put our hands over our mouths so we wouldn't laugh. Mister Adams laughed out loud, like it was the funniest thing he'd ever heard.

Professor Tuesday stopped in front of a row of buildings. Some looked to be houses. Most of them were made of wood. A few of them were built with bricks or stone. Laundry was hung over ropes on the porches. Besides houses, some of the other buildings looked like stores. People went in and often came out with baskets full of goods or bundles tied with brown string.

Rachel and I were interested in seeing the different clothing people wore in this frontier town. Everywhere you looked there was something different. Even though it was a warm day, most women wore long dresses. None of them wore shorts or pants. Many of the women had bonnets on their heads. Some of the men wore white shirts with ties and a jacket. Boys ran in the street wearing short pants. We thought everybody dressed funny.

Still, there was much more to see in Detroit.

The Pothole

Detroit—July 1837

As we walked by a narrow alley, we saw children playing with a ball. They were batting it around with sticks in the dirt, chasing back and forth.

"Looks like they're playing hockey," Owen said. "I play on a travel team."

"I don't think they are playing hockey," Rachel said. "Get real, Owen."

The professor stopped and pointed toward the far end of the main street. "Over 150 years from now, the Joe Louis Arena will be built right there."

"That's where the Red Wings play, isn't it?" Owen asked.

"Yes, it is," answered the professor.

Suddenly a big ruckus broke out down the street. We ran to see what was going on. A man with a bandanna on his head was having a problem. The cart he was pushing down the street was stuck in a deep rut. He was blocking traffic in the road, and people were yelling at him. No matter how hard the man pushed, the cart wouldn't budge.

Rachel and I watched Mister Adams as Owen and Professor Tuesday went over to help. They put their backs to the cart as the man pulled from the front. After some pushing and shoving, the cart was out of the rut.

"Danke," said the man.

"Gern geschehen," said Professor Tuesday.

"What was that?" I asked.

"He said 'thank you' and I said 'you are welcome' in German," answered the professor.

"Cool," Owen said. "AH-H-H-CHOOO!"

"Gesundheit," Professor Tuesday said with a big smile. "That means 'good health' in German."

As we walked off, a man came out of a house and started yelling at the professor. He was really, really mad about something. The professor tried his best to calm him down. Though we couldn't understand what Professor Tuesday was saying, it appeared as though he was telling the man he was sorry. Before long, the man stomped off back into his house.

"Oops," said the professor, "I forgot."

Mister Adams ran up to him and hugged the professor's knees.

The professor patted his nephew on the head. "Its okay, Mister Adams."

"What's wrong, Professor?" Owen asked.

Professor Tuesday rubbed the back of his neck as he explained. "You see, in the 1800s the streets in Detroit had a lot of potholes. The people who lived near big ruts, like the one back there, claimed the right to help pull wagons out of the mud for a price. So, when we helped that German fellow get his wagon out of the mud, the property owner got angry because he lost a chance to make some extra money."

"Crazy," said Owen. "You're telling me that people actually owned the potholes in front of their houses, and they got paid for helping push wagons out of them?"

"That's right," said the professor. "It's kind of like owning a tow truck business in our time."

"I've got an uncle who lives in Utica," Rachel said. "He claims they've got potholes there that can eat an entire car."

We laughed as we continued our walk through the frontier town of Detroit. Rachel took careful notes of everything she saw and heard. Owen mostly drew pictures in his journal. Now and then I looked over to make sure Mister Adams was following us. He was being very good. Maybe babysitting him wouldn't be too bad after all.

Professor Tuesday stopped in front of another building and looked inside. Smoke poured out of a chimney on the roof. The professor waved us over to take a look. Heat from inside the building washed over us as we got near the door. Men with long aprons were working by a furnace. Others were pounding metal into shape and working on large pieces of steel. The metal was red hot and they were using big hammers to make it into a circular shape. Glowing sparks flew with each strike of their hammers.

"We'd better be going now. There are other places I want to visit today. Before we leave, let's take a look at that building," the professor said as he crossed the street.

The State Building

Detroit—July 1837

As we walked along, Owen stepped on one of his loose shoelaces and tripped over Mister Adams.

Professor Tuesday ran to Owen's side. "Are you alright?" he asked.

Owen picked himself up. "I'm fine. It seems like I fall a lot." Owen bent down and tied his loose shoelaces.

"It's because you are a clumsy oaf," Rachel said. "And your shoes are always untied."

Owen gave Rachel an angry stare.

"Now, now," said the professor. "Let's try to get along here."

We walked toward a large building outside of town. Professor Tuesday shrugged his shoulders twice as he continued. "There are many reasons I wanted you to see Detroit in 1837. Besides seeing immigrants coming to Michigan, 1837 was the year that Michigan became a state."

The professor pointed to a building. "That building is the capitol building of Michigan. It was built in 1828. Back then people complained that the capitol building was too far from town. However, the city grew rapidly as immigrants poured into the state searching for opportunity."

"I thought the state capital was in Lansing?" Rachel asked.

"It is in our time," replied the professor. "It was moved from Detroit to Lansing in 1848." The professor scratched his chin and looked over at Owen as he thought. "I'll bet you didn't know that Michigan had a boy governor in 1837."

"Really?" Owen asked.

"Yes, his name was Stevens T. Mason," answered the professor. "He was named the Territorial Secretary by President Andrew Jackson when he was only nineteen years old. He became Michigan's first elected governor in 1835 when he was only twenty-four."

The professor stopped walking for a moment. "When Mason was the Territorial Secretary, he did a lot to encourage immigrants to come to Michigan. The U.S. government required that a territory have at least 60,000 settlers before it would consider the territory to become a state. Partially because of population growth and partially because of the boy governor's efforts, Michigan became a state in 1837."

"Maybe I could be the governor some day," Owen said proudly.

"You'd have to stop being such a nerd first," Rachel shot back.

"Rachel! Would you just cool it?" I said.

Suddenly, we heard some shouting. It was coming from down the street. A crowd of people quickly gathered. Mister Adams headed off to investigate, and we all followed. The professor's nephew worked his way through the noisy crowd to see what was happening.

In the middle of the ring of people, two men were wrestling around on the ground. Back and forth they went. The crowd shouted to them in different languages. As the fight went on, one of the men broke free and picked up a rock that had been in the dirt road. The noisy crowd went silent. Everyone realized that the argument had turned very dangerous.

The fighters circled each other cautiously. The man with the rock held it above his head, ready to strike. Then, something amazing happened. A woman in a dirty apron pushed her way through the crowd and walked right up to the man with the rock. I couldn't understand what she said to him, but she grabbed his ear and twisted it. The man dropped the rock instantly, and everyone laughed as the woman led him away by his ear.

Professor Tuesday smiled broadly. "As you can see, immigrants didn't always get along with each other. Different customs and ways of life caused problems." The professor stopped and looked directly at Owen and Rachel. "Sooner or later we all have to learn to get along."

As we walked we saw some strange looking buildings. There were warehouses, homes, and stores right next to each other.

It seemed like Professor Tuesday knew what I was thinking. "Homes, stores, and hotels were often built right next door to each other. They didn't have malls back then."

"Animals wandering around all over the place and no malls," Rachel said. "I'm glad I didn't live in Michigan in 1837."

"Business was booming in Detroit back then," said the professor. "There were also hotels and boarding houses in Detroit in 1837. With so many immigrants coming to and through Detroit, they needed places to stay while they conducted their business."

"What kind of business did people do in Detroit?" Rachel asked.

"Well," answered the professor, "People would go to deposit money at the banks. These deposits were usually used to purchase land at a later date. Plus, the land office was a very popular place for people who wanted to settle in Michigan."

"Didn't the native people own the land?" Rachel asked.

"It would seem so," said Professor Tuesday. "However, treaties and agreements were made with tribes throughout the territory to purchase land.

"I'm surprised to see all those farms outside of town and around the capitol building. That's strange," Owen noted.

"Many farms in and around Detroit in the early 1800s were owned by the French," said Professor Tuesday. "Some of the early French men married Native American women. Those marriages often helped them establish good relationships with local Native Americans. That way, they could farm or trade furs in peace."

"Professor, can we visit some immigrant settlements now?" I asked

"Yes we can," the professor answered. "I think we should visit the settlements of the Franconians."

"I thought we were going to visit a settlement of Germans," Rachel said. "Who are the Franconians?"

"We shall see," said the professor with a smile, "we shall see."

As we headed back to the Tuesday Teleporter, Mister Adams took off after a chicken that was wandering around in the street. The chicken ran in circles with the professor's nephew close behind. Mister Adams was fast, but the chicken was faster. It was a very funny sight.

We took a look around Detroit in 1837 one last time before we stepped back through the teleporter.

The Franconians
Frankenmuth—July 1855

Once we got back to the professor's office, he took cheese sticks out of his desk and offered one to each of us. Then he set to work programming our next trip into his computer. "We will be visiting Frankenmuth next," he said.

"Traveling through time sure makes me hungry," Owen said. Mister Adams gave him a big thumbs-up.

After the shower of lights and sounds filled the room, the green cloud formed once again. "Let's go," said the professor. Then he stopped suddenly. "Oh, heavens, I almost forgot." The professor quickly returned to his desk and opened the top drawer. He reached inside and grabbed some strange looking objects. He adjusted each of the objects before putting one over his ear. Then he put one on Mister

Adams before handing one to me, one to Rachel, and another to Owen.

"My dad uses one of these when he's driving and wants to talk on his cell phone," Rachel said. "You know, my father is a doctor."

"Yes, I remember you told me that during your last visit," said the professor. "You are very smart. And, yes, this does look like one of those devices people use to talk on cell phones. However, these are Tuesday Translators. Put them over your ears and they will translate other languages to English. They will also translate whatever you say into different languages. I have adjusted them so that we will all be able to understand and speak German."

The professor turned to his desk once more. He came back with a piece of rope. He tied one end around Rachel's middle and the other around Mister Adams. "Now," the professor said to Rachel, "it's your turn to watch Mister Adams. This time it will be harder for him to wander off."

Finally, we went through the teleporter once again.

After our tumbling ride, we stepped out of the green cloud and into a swampy area near a river. A Native American woman saw us from the other side of the river and ran away. I think we scared her. Her screams scared us, too. Professor Tuesday had us crouch down quietly for a few minutes. I wasn't worried at all. However, Owen looked frightened.

We waited for a while, then the professor took out his compass and he pulled an old map out of his pocket. He unfolded it carefully and placed the compass on it. Professor Tuesday turned himself until the needle on the compass pointed to the north mark.

"Do you think we are in trouble with the native people?" Owen asked.

"No," said the professor as he looked up from his map, "the Chippewa Indians who live in this area are usually friendly. I think we just scared her a little, that's all. This way," the professor said, as he pointed away from the river.

We followed the professor. The rope around Rachel's waist tightened. She turned to find Mister Adams throwing rocks into the river.

"C'mon, Mister Adams," she said. "We need to follow the professor." The professor's nephew scowled and started walking along with us.

In a short time, we came to a farm field. Rows of plants were growing in the dark soil. A woman and three children were hoeing weeds from around the plants. They looked up when we approached. One of the children shouted something as he pointed toward us, and the woman spoke to them.

The Tuesday Translator in my ear sparked to life. "Look, mother," a young-sounding voice echoed, "there are some other children. Can we play?"

Though she spoke in a language I didn't know, I understood everything she said. "Children, we have much work to do. There is no time for play."

The family went back to work as we continued our journey through early Frankenmuth. At the far end of the field, men were building a log home. They were cutting long logs with axes and saws. Then they fit the pieces together to make walls. With a new log in place, they packed mud between the logs to fill in the empty spaces. It looked like hard work.

Behind the men was a small building standing all by itself. I wondered what it was. Thick forests surrounded each of the farms we passed. I guess we walked by three or four farms before we came upon a finished log building. A man stood out in front talking with two Native Americans. I couldn't hear what they were saying because they were too far away. The man talking to the two native people was dressed in a black suit with a white shirt and black tie. He wore a black hat even though it was warm outside.

The professor raised his fingers to his lips. "Sh-h-h," he whispered. "Let's stay here and watch what happens."

We stood together in the shade of a grove of trees. Birds flew overhead and insects danced in the air. Not much was happening. The native people walked away and the man who was talking with them went into the building. Professor Tuesday signaled us that it was time to do a little more exploring.

We started walking away, but Rachel was stopped by the rope around her middle. When she turned back to tell Mister Adams to follow us, she was surprised.

Somehow Mister Adams had untied himself while we were watching the man and the native people. While we weren't paying attention to him, he tied his end of the rope around a tree. When Rachel started walking away, she couldn't go very far. The two of us looked around carefully as the professor and Owen started off. However, we didn't see Mister Adams anywhere.

"Oh, no, Professor," my friend said. "Mister Adams untied himself. Now he's gone again."

Professor Tuesday looked shocked when he saw that Mister Adams had taken off his rope and tied it to a tree. We all quickly looked through the woods we were hiding in, but we couldn't see the professor's nephew anywhere.

"I'm sorry," Rachel said to the professor. "I thought he was standing by me all the time."

"That little stinker sure is smart," said the professor. "I am not angry with you, I'm upset with Mister Adams. Though it is not too dangerous here, we must find him quickly. The Tuesday Teleporter will only stay open so long. If it closes before we get back, we'll be stuck in this time."

"I don't like the sound of that," said Owen. Rachel and I nodded our heads in agreement.

We scanned the nearby countryside. "We weren't here that long," said the professor. "He can't be far."

We looked up in the trees first. The last time we lost Mister Adams, he had climbed a tree. But, he wasn't in any of the trees nearby. Suddenly, Owen noticed something.

"Look," he said as he pointed down, "I found some footprints. They're small, so they must be Mister Adams's."

"Let's see where they take us," said the professor.

The footprints seemed to be heading back the way we came.

After a long, hard search, we found Mister Adams at the very first farm field we passed in the settlement. He was helping the children pull weeds. His hands and clothes were dirty, and his face was covered in mud. A young boy was working in the field next to the professor's nephew.

The professor spoke to the boy. The Tuesday Translator changed the professor's words so the boy could understand. "Thank you for taking care of my nephew."

The words that came out of his mouth were strange to me, but my earpiece told me what he said. The boy said, "You are welcome. Pulling weeds is no fun, but we made a game of it. Your nephew was very helpful."

The professor took Mister Adams by the hand and gave him a stern look. After a short walk, we all made it back to the teleporter, safe and sound.

Time-Out

The Professor's Office—Today

When we returned to the professor's office, he put his hands on his hips and scolded his nephew. "Now, Mister Adams, you can't be wandering off like that. I am very upset with you. You could have been lost or hurt. Your mother would be very angry if that happened. So, I'm going to put you in TIME-OUT so you can think about what you have done."

The professor marched his little nephew over to the corner and pulled up a chair for him. "Now, you stay here. When you've been in TIME-OUT for ten minutes, you can come over and join us."

Mister Adams gave Professor Tuesday an angry look as he took his seat facing the corner. The rest of us gathered around the table in the professor's office. Owen, Rachel, and I covered our mouths and tried not to giggle out loud.

"Now," said the professor, "let's talk about Frankenmuth." The professor shifted in his seat and peeked over to make certain Mister Adams was still in TIME-OUT. "As I said before, there were several German settlements in Michigan. The earliest immigrants from Germany built farms and businesses in and around Detroit, Ann Arbor, and Monroe. Frankenmuth, however, has some very interesting history. The first settlers to Frankenmuth left German soil in April of 1845. The trip across the Atlantic Ocean lasted nine weeks, and it was very dangerous."

"Like how?" Owen asked.

The professor doodled on a piece of paper with a pencil as he answered. "Well, for several days they sailed through thick fog in the middle of some icebergs."

"Like the *Titanic*?" I gasped.

"Yes," said the professor, "traveling across the Atlantic Ocean was very dangerous for many immigrants. The ships were often crowded and uncomfortable. Many of the travelers didn't have enough food for the voyage, some even died from diseases."

"Like the flu?" Rachel asked. "Many of my father's patients have the flu."

"There were many diseases aboard the ships. Some of them were quite deadly."

"That must have been terrible," Owen said.

The professor nodded his head. "The people who came to settle Frankenmuth first arrived in New York City in June 1845. After months of traveling, they arrived in Saginaw, then they took another boat down the Saginaw River to their settlement on the Cass River. Within a few days, the village of Frankenmuth started to take shape." The professor put his pencil down and looked at us. "I'm curious about what you saw on our visit to Frankenmuth?" the professor asked as he scratched his hairy chin. "What did you write in your journals?"

"Before that," Rachel said, "you told us that we were going to visit the Franconees ... or something like that, but my dad told me that Frankenmuth was a German settlement."

"Yes and no," answered Professor Tuesday. "Germany wasn't recognized as a country until about 1871. So, people who came from that part of the world didn't consider themselves as German before that time. The people who settled Frankenmuth were actually Franconians. Franconia is a region in Bavaria in Germany. The word *Frankenmuth* actually means 'courage of the Franconians.'"

"Aren't there other places around there with the word 'Franken' in them? Like Frankenstein or something?" Owen asked.

The professor wrinkled his brow and chuckled. "Why yes, there is Frankentrost, Frankenlust, and even a Frankenhilf. All of them were established in the Saginaw Valley. Frankenmuth was the first settlement in the area. But, there was no Frankenstein."

"That's kind of funny," I said, "but I also think it's funny to give your new home the same name as your old home."

"Frankenmuth wasn't the only community of Germans that did that," the professor said as he adjusted his glasses twice. "The community of West-phalia was built on the west side of the state on the Grand River. It was originally settled by people from Westphalia in what is now Germany."

"I have another question about Frankenmuth," Owen said. "Why did the Franconians move there in the first place? It was in the middle of nowhere."

"Good question," said Professor Tuesday. "Their original purpose for moving to Michigan was to be missionaries to the Chippewa Indians who lived in the Saginaw Valley. The Franconians purchased 680 acres of land for $2.50 an acre."

"You said 'original purpose'," I noted. "Did something happen?"

"The families spent almost all their time building homes and farms. They really didn't do much else. As for the minister, he was a bit hardheaded. I read in a book that the Franconian minister expected the Chippewa people to come to him. He didn't travel to meet them. So he probably wasn't a very good missionary after all."

"Near the log building there was a man talking to some Native Americans. Do you think he was the minister?" Rachel asked.

"I do," said the professor. "And, the building he was standing in front of was the first church in the community. It was called St. Lorenz. The church is still there today, but not the original building."

"The farms were pretty," Owen said. "And some guys were building something."

"I think they were building a farmhouse," said Professor Tuesday. "The farms the Franconians built in Michigan were different from the farms they had back in Europe. In the old country, farmers lived in villages. Their farmland was usually outside the villages. Each day they would travel from their homes to work at their farms. The settlers in Frankenmuth chose to farm like most Americans did, living right on their farmland."

"What was that little building near the house they were building?" Rachel asked.

"It was probably the outhouse," answered the professor.

"What's that?" Owen asked.

"Back then people didn't have bathrooms like we do in our time. They didn't even have electricity, running water, plumbing, or flush toilets. So, they dug pits into the ground and put outhouses over them."

"O-O-Oh," said Owen.

"Gross," said Rachel.

The professor thought for a moment before continuing. "Did you notice how big the trees were in the forest and how the farms were cleared out of the woods?"

We nodded our heads.

"When the people of Frankenmuth first arrived, the whole state was covered in trees. They had to cut down trees and clear the land before they could even plant crops. None of the trees they cut down went to waste. They were used to build the church, homes, and barns of the community. In many communities, immigrants would share a house with someone who already had one until theirs could be built. In other situations, they would live in mud huts, sometimes tents."

"I like camping," I said, "but I don't think I'd like living in a mud hut or a tent for a long time."

Professor Tuesday took a peek at Mister Adams. He could tell his nephew wasn't happy about being in TIME-OUT. Then the professor asked another question. "Do you recall seeing the pigpen on our visit?"

"Were the Franconians good pig farmers?" Owen asked.

"Pigs were pretty important to many early settlers to Michigan. The forest around Frankenmuth had a lot of oak trees. Pigs were fed acorns from the oak trees, so the farmers had a good supply of food for pigs."

"I'll bet they also had chickens," Rachel said. "My grandma and grandpa love to take us out for chicken dinners in Frankenmuth."

"I'm sure they had chickens," answered the professor with a chuckle.

"What crops did they grow on their farms?" Owen asked.

"Mister Adams was helping to pull weeds in a potato field. The early Franconians also grew some cabbage and beets during the first years of the settlement," the professor added.

Just then, the professor thought about his nephew in TIME-OUT. He turned to take a look at Mister Adams. Professor Tuesday's nephew was writing on the wall with a crayon. When he noticed that the professor was looking at him, Mister Adams put his finger by his nose and twisted his hand.

The professor laughed out loud. "Mister Adams says he's bored. Maybe we should take another quick trip before we have lunch."

He didn't seem to mind that his nephew had written all over his office wall with a crayon. "You can come out of TIME-OUT now, Mister Adams. But you must not run off again."

Mister Adams nodded his head in agreement and climbed down from his chair. He crossed the room and joined us at the table. He seemed to be happy that he was no longer sitting in the corner.

"What are we going to see next?" I asked.

"Can we visit Polish immigrants?" Owen asked. "Rachel got to visit Germans. Now it's my turn. Can we visit the Polish, please, Professor?"

"Not just yet," said the professor, "I want you to see something else first."

The Dutch
Holland, Michigan—June 1849

We got ready for our third trip of the day into history. I was eager to find out where the professor was taking us. When he returned from taking a peek into the past, his hair and beard were all messed up. After he straightened himself, we stepped through the green cloud. Before long, we were standing on the top of some sand dunes. A big, beautiful lake was off in the distance behind us.

"It's very windy today in Holland, Michigan," the professor said.

"Are we really in Holland?" Rachel shouted above the wind. "Cool, I can't wait to see the tulips and windmills. My dad even bought me a pair of wooden shoes here when I was little."

The professor just smiled and winked twice. "I don't think we'll be seeing any tulips, windmills, or wooden shoes. The Dutch have only been here a couple of years. It's 1849. So, what we see today won't look much like the Holland, Michigan, of our time."

Sand whipped at our backs as Professor Tuesday pulled out his trusty compass. Then he started walking away from the lake and dunes. This time, we all kept a careful eye on Mister Adams. We didn't want to lose him again.

Once we got away from the sand dunes, the ground got mucky and swampy. Owen stopped to tie his shoes tightly.

"I don't want my shoes to come off," he said with a weak smile.

"Good thinking," said Professor Tuesday.

"AH-H-H ...," Owen started to sneeze again, but he plugged his nose just in time.

The farther away we got from the lake and the dunes, the calmer the wind was. We picked our way carefully through the damp, soggy ground and came to a small wooden building. The professor made sure that our Tuesday Translators were on and working. He turned a small knob on each translator so we could speak and understand Dutch. As we peeked into the window, we saw several children inside, seated at benches. The girls wore dark dresses and had bonnets on their heads. The boys wore knee-length pants and white shirts.

"It's a school," I whispered.

"That's right," Professor Tuesday added quietly. "Let's listen in for a while."

We were surprised to hear English. The teacher was giving a lesson on the alphabet. Each child held a small blackboard and wrote letters with chalk. After the alphabet lesson was over, the teacher spoke in Dutch. Our Tuesday Translators went to work changing the Dutch words into English so we could understand. The class started working on arithmetic … addition and subtraction.

"Yuck," Owen said softly, "I don't like math."

"Maybe you'd learn to like math if you did your homework for a change," scolded Rachel.

Soon, the professor waved for us to follow him, and we continued exploring. Thick, tall pine trees were everywhere. A strong, woodsy smell filled the air. Mister Adams skipped along as we came to the shore of a smaller lake. We watched a beaver swim out in the water. It carried a long branch in its mouth.

We followed the shoreline until we came to a clearing. Men were chopping down a tree at the far side. Their axes made loud "thunking" sounds as they dug into the giant tree.

"Watch this," said the professor.

After a few more swings of the axe, the huge tree started making a loud, crunching sound. The men who were cutting the tree quickly grabbed their tools and ran away. Slowly at first, the tree started tipping. Mister Adams put his hands over his ears. When the tree fell, it made a terrible noise as it hit the ground. The earth shook under our feet.

"Whoa," Owen said, "that was awesome."

The men came out of the woods with their tools and began cutting the limbs off the tree and moving them into large piles. We watched for a while before the professor motioned for us to keep moving.

At the far end of the lake we saw a field with some crops growing in neat rows. A crude log house sat at the edge of the lake. A man and woman were working in a small garden near the house. We walked along the field, careful not to step on any plants.

As we passed by the farm house, the professor waved at the man and woman. They waved back, then quickly returned to their work. Mister Adams liked to wave at the people, but we took him by the hand and continued our walk.

"Just a little farther," said the professor as he looked around to make sure Mister Adams was still nearby. The professor pointed toward his nephew. Mister Adams was watching a butterfly fluttering to and fro through the wildflowers in a small clearing.

After we left the field, we came upon a well-worn path that ran east and west. The professor sat on a log, pulled out his pocketknife, and whittled on a stick. Then he started drawing in the dirt with the sharpened end. Professor Tuesday drew a quick map of where we'd been on our trip to Holland in 1849. He pointed out the big lake, the dunes, the schoolhouse, the smaller lake, the place where the men cut down the tree, the farm, and where we were now resting. I wrote some notes in my journal. Owen scribbled a few pictures in his.

"Is that all there is to see here?" I asked.

"No," answered the professor, "I want to rest for a while along this path. Perhaps we'll meet someone."

Just after the professor finished speaking, a man came around a bend on the trail. He was carrying a large bundle and heading toward the town of Holland.

"Good afternoon, sir," the professor said. His Tuesday Translator changed the words into Dutch so the man could understand him. "Sit down and join us for a short rest."

"Good afternoon," the man said in Dutch as he lowered his bundle and took a seat on the log. He took off his cap and wiped his brow before speaking. "It is a long walk from Grand Rapids. I am glad to be near my home."

"Looks like you purchased some supplies," the professor said.

"Yes," said the man, "some food items, a few small tools, and some fishing hooks."

"How's the fishing?" Owen asked.

The man smiled. "We catch many fish. My family lives on the fish we catch and small game we hunt. Sometimes my children tell me they are tired of eating fish all the time, so I bought some vegetables for them. I also purchased some seed. This year we will grow our own vegetables."

"Did you see any native people?" I asked.

"No," said the man as he gathered up his bundle. "We do not see many native people here." The man lifted his bundle and wished us a good day as he walked off.

"I think it's time we be heading back as well," said the professor. "We have much to talk about."

Owen Takes a Trip
The Professor's Office—Today

We followed the path back toward the village of Holland. As we walked, Owen tripped on a tree root and fell flat on his face. When he got up, his lip was bleeding and his glasses were bent. Mister Adams ran to his side and started wiping the dirt off of his shirt.

"Are you alright?" the professor asked as he rushed to Owen's side.

"He's fine," Rachel said. "Owen falls down all the time. Like I said before, he doesn't always tie his shoes, and he's clumsy. He doesn't get good grades like I do either."

Owen steamed as he looked at Rachel. Then she started up again. "I don't know why you're staring at me. Everything I said was true. You're always a mess, and I am always neat and tidy, just ask my mom."

The professor made sure Owen was okay, then we continued down the path. Before long, we were back at the sand dunes. We stepped through the green cloud and tumbled back through time to the professor's office.

Professor Tuesday went down the hall and got a wet towel for Owen. As my classmate cleaned himself up, we started talking about what we had seen in early Holland, Michigan.

"Professor," I asked, "why did Dutch people migrate to Michigan in the first place?"

"There are always many reasons why people immigrate to a new place," said the professor. "The Dutch first came to Michigan in 1847 for religious reasons. They didn't like some of the things that were going on in their home country. They thought that if they moved to America, they could preserve their culture and their own religious beliefs. Our visit to them took place about two years after they first arrived."

"Were they missionaries like the Germans were in Frankenmuth?" Owen asked as he wiped his face.

"Yes and no," said the professor as he scribbled some notes on a piece of paper. "Some of their early documents and speeches told of their plans to be missionaries. But, like the Germans in Frankenmuth, they really didn't do much to spread their religion once they started their settlement."

"The school was pretty cool," said Owen. "They spoke both English and Dutch there."

"Very good, my friend," nodded Professor Tuesday, "you were paying attention."

"He doesn't always do that in class. That's why he's always in trouble," Rachel said.

Owen hung his head, "Nobody's perfect, not even you, Rachel."

Professor Tuesday looked at Rachel as Miss Pepper does every once in a while, then he spoke. "Schoolhouses in those days had only one or two windows. A door was on one end of the building, and a fireplace or wood-burning stove was at the other. During the first few years of the settlement, the Dutch hired a teacher. Their children were given lessons in both English and Dutch."

"Why?" I asked.

"Well, it seems as though the Dutch wanted to preserve their culture and language. At the same time, they wanted their children to learn English, the language of their new country."

"I saw the children writing on little chalk-boards," Owen said. "Didn't they have paper in those days?"

"They did have paper," answered the professor, "but it was far too expensive to be used in school. Children often practiced writing with chalk on pieces of slate. When they were done with their lessons, they would wipe the slate with a cloth or their sleeves. In some of the poorer areas of the state, children would use sticks and practice their writing in sand or dirt."

"When we arrived, there was a big lake on the other side of the sand dunes. After we visited the school, we walked by another lake," I said. "What were those lakes?"

"Remember the map I drew in the dirt?" asked the professor. "Well, the lake on the other side of the sand dunes from us was Lake Michigan. The smaller lake we saw was called Black Lake back then. The name was later changed to Lake Macatawa."

The professor thought for a minute before he continued. "You may be interested in learning that the French had an influence in how some of the lakes in and around Michigan were named. The French use the word *lake* before the name of a body of water, like Lake Michigan. The Great Lakes all use the word *lake* before the name of the lake. Other lakes in the state, such as Higgins Lake, Wixom Lake, and Houghton Lake, do not because they didn't use French naming for those lakes."

"I never knew that," Owen said. "That's pretty cool. You know what I liked, professor? I liked seeing that tree get chopped down by those guys."

"Just like in Frankenmuth, the Dutch had to cut down trees in order to clear farmland and build houses," said the professor. Rachel wrote notes as the professor continued. "From what I've read, they weren't very good loggers when they first came to Michigan."

"What do you mean?" Owen asked.

"In the Netherlands, they didn't have huge forests with tall trees like Michigan did. Cutting down trees is no easy job, and it's dangerous. Several Dutch settlers were injured very badly cutting down trees. Some were even killed."

Owen's eyes got really big. "People were killed chopping down trees? No way!"

"Way," answered Professor Tuesday. "Those trees were very tall and very heavy. Did you feel the ground shake when it fell?"

We nodded our heads silently.

Mister Adams gestured to the professor in sign language. The professor watched closely, then spoke, "Mister Adams wants to know what the farmers were growing in the field."

He thought for a while, trying to remember exactly what the farm field looked like. "I think they were growing celery, but I can't be sure. Dutch farmers usually grew crops like celery and onions. The soil in the Holland area is rich with silt from the river systems, making it good for producing crops for food and trade."

"The man we saw on the path said he bought some food, tools, and some fishing hooks," I said. "Didn't his crops do well?"

"Not necessarily," answered the professor. "He may have just started his farm. Some families lived in huts or shelters made from tree branches while they cleared enough land for a farm, just like in Frankenmuth and other settlements. The winters were much colder and windier in Michigan than in the Netherlands, which made life in the New World very difficult for the Dutch. They needed to trade for some items and the closest place to trade was Grand Rapids ... a distance of twenty miles or more."

"He walked all that way?" asked Owen.

"Yes, he did," said the professor. "Most early immigrants didn't own horses, so they walked wherever they needed to go."

Mister Adams made the sign that he was hungry.

"I am hungry, too," said the professor. "Let's talk over lunch. I've written down some notes that you may want to include in your report. Bring your journals and pencils—this will be fun."

Foreign Food
The University Cafeteria—Today

It was a nice walk from the professor's office to the university cafeteria. It wasn't as windy as Holland or as cool as Frankenmuth. Though Rachel kept sniping at Owen, I was enjoying myself. I also enjoyed being around Mister Adams. He is one funny little dude.

My thoughts were interrupted when Owen sneezed, "AH-H-H-CHOO!" Then he said, "Excuse me."

"Bless you," said the professor.

"See, Professor," Rachel said, "Owen is always tripping and sneezing and stuff."

"I think Owen said it best," added the professor, "nobody's perfect." The professor rubbed Owen's head.

At the cafeteria we each took a tray. "I'm treating everyone to lunch today," said the professor kindly. "Choose whatever you'd like as long as it is healthy."

The cafeteria had a special island with just Mexican food. That's Owens favorite kind of food. I went to the pasta bar because I love Italian food. Rachel got some Chinese stir-fry. The professor had his usual lunch, a tuna fish sandwich cut in two and two hard-boiled eggs. Mister Adams ordered a peanut-butter-and-jelly sandwich on toast and a big, juicy dill pickle. Everything looked very good, and we were all hungry. As we were picking out our lunches, I thought about one of the wonderful things that immigrants have given us—different kinds of food.

We all took a seat at a table at the back of the cafeteria. The table was by a window that looked over the university campus. It was nice and quiet, perfect for having a pleasant talk.

Before Owen started eating, he said, "Thank you for lunch, Professor."

Mister Adams said "thank you" in sign language.

"Yes, thank you," I added. When Rachel didn't say anything, I kicked her leg under the table.

"Oh, yah, thanks Professor," Rachel added.

"You're all very welcome."

Before Mister Adams started to eat his sandwich, the professor took a knife and sliced his nephew's pickle. What happened next almost made Rachel and me hurl. Mister Adams took his sandwich apart and put pickle slices on top of the peanut butter and jelly.

"Is he really going to eat a peanut-butter-and-jelly sandwich with pickles on it?" Rachel asked as she scrunched up her face.

"Yuck," I said.

Then Owen spoke up, "I'd be willing to give it a try."

The professor just chuckled and said, "To each his own."

As we munched on our food, the professor asked us questions. "What things were the same in the German and Dutch settlements we visited?"

"Well," Owen said between bites of his taco, "both had farms and farmers."

"That's true," said the professor as he peeled one of his eggs. "Farming was and is an important job. Early settlers relied on farming plus fishing and hunting for their food. The Germans grew common crops that were big parts of their diets, like beets, potatoes, and cabbage. The Dutch tended to grow specialty crops that could be used for trade, like celery and onions. What immigrants couldn't make, grow, shoot, or catch, they had to get through trade or purchase."

"That's right," I said. "That one Dutch guy had to walk all the way to Grand Rapids and back just to pick up a few supplies. I don't think I could do that."

The professor agreed. "There weren't grocery stores nearby like we have today, so farming was a common job for immigrants for many, many years."

"So," Rachel noted, "the immigrants who first came to Michigan were all farmers?"

"Not all," said the professor. "Some were also craftsmen and shopkeepers. Opening up a new territory or a state offered plenty of opportunity for people who were willing to work hard and build a business. Though not all immigrants were successful, many were able to make a good living."

The professor took a bite of his tuna fish sandwich and continued, "So, what other things were the same with the two communities?"

"Both of them immigrated to Michigan for religious reasons," Rachel said smartly.

Mister Adams pointed one finger up, and another toward her, then brought them together.

"Mister Adams says you are right," the professor noted. "Very good, Mister Adams, and very good, Rachel, you are correct. Both the Dutch and the Germans did move to Michigan for religious reasons. The Germans moved to Frankenmuth in order to be missionaries to the Chippewa Indians. The Dutch established a home in Holland, Michigan, in order to preserve their religion and culture."

We ate silently for a while. Mister Adams was making yummy sounds as he enjoyed his sandwich. The crunching sound the pickle made as he bit into his peanut-butter-and-jelly and pickle sandwich made me shiver. He was wearing a big streak of jelly on his face. The professor took a napkin and gently wiped his nephew's face.

"Any other similarities?" the professor asked.

Owen spoke up once again, "There were lots of big trees in both places. And, it looked like they had to be cut down to make room for farms and buildings."

"Right you are," said the professor. "In those days Michigan looked very different than it does today. Very large, old trees covered much of the state."

"What happened to them?" I asked.

"Almost all of those trees were cut down during the lumbering era in Michigan," answered the professor. "The hardwood trees in the Holland and Grand Rapids area—such as oak, maple, and walnut—were important to establish Grand Rapids as a city known for furniture building.

"What's a lumbering era?" Rachel asked.

"From about the mid-1800s until the early 1900s, lumber companies in Michigan hired thousands of immigrants to cut down trees and saw the tree trunks into lumber. These trees were used to build houses and furniture."

Professor Tuesday drew a mitten shape on a piece of paper. "Imagine that this is the Lower Peninsula of Michigan," the professor said. Then he drew a line from the basin of Saginaw Bay over somewhere toward Muskegon. "Land south of this line is mostly made up of good, fertile soil that is useful for farming. Hardwood trees grew mostly in this southern area of the Lower Peninsula. The northern part of the Lower Peninsula and the entire Upper Peninsula of Michigan are made up of mostly sandy soil that isn't ideal for farming. But, it is very good for growing pine trees."

Without another word, the professor stood up and left the table. When he returned, he was carrying big bowls of ice cream with fudge sauce, one for each of us. Mister Adams clapped his hands in delight. We all said thanks one more time before digging into the treats.

"Now, where was I?" asked the professor. "Oh, yes, I was talking about the lumbering era. The best trees for building were pines. The most valuable of all the trees were white pines. Some called them cork pines because the best trees floated like corks in the river. Most of these beautiful trees have been gone from Michigan for some time. But, you can find out more about them at Hartwick Pines State Park, north of Grayling, Michigan." Professor Tuesday thought for a moment. "Maybe we should see some of the lumbering era immigrants this afternoon."

Then the professor turned to Mister Adams. "Before I forget, I just want to say how proud I am of Mister Adams for paying attention and not wandering off during our last trip back in time." The professor patted his nephew on the head, "Thank you, you were very good."

Mister Adams said "you're welcome" in sign language.

The professor finished the last of his tuna fish sandwich in two bites and then asked another question. "We talked about things that were the same, what were some of the things that were different between the two settlements?"

"They spoke different languages," Owen said.

"Duh," Rachel replied, "no kidding."

"Owen made a good point," said the professor. "Though the Dutch and German languages can sound somewhat similar, they aren't the same. There are even different words and manners of speech within each language." The professor paused for a moment. "Were there any other differences in the two colonies?"

"The Dutch colony had a school, we didn't see one in Frankenmuth," Rachel said, as she read through her journal notes.

"The German community did build a school in connection with the church very soon after the settlement was established," noted the professor. "Did you notice anything else?"

"I know! I know!" Owen said excitedly. "We saw Native Americans near Frankenmuth. But the man on the path near Holland said they didn't have many native people. That's a difference, isn't it?"

The professor jumped up from the table and danced around. "Very, very good! There were Native Americans living near Frankenmuth ... mostly Chippewa Indians. However, very few native people lived near Holland. Do you know why?"

Owen and Mister Adams shrugged and shook their heads.

"In 1821 three tribes, the Potawatomi, Chippewa, and the Ottawa signed a treaty in which they gave up their claims to all land in Michigan south of the Grand River. In exchange for their land, the Native American tribes were paid $5,000 a year for twenty years. Plus, they were given $1,000 a year for a blacksmith and a teacher."

"So, the Grand River is north of Holland?" I asked. "That's why they didn't see Native Americans very often."

"Right," said the professor. "We've all learned a lot today. Are you ready for some more?"

"Yes!" Owen, Rachel, and I shouted together. Mister Adams made a fist with his hand then bent his wrist up and down.

"That means yes," the professor said with a wide smile. "It sounds like we should get back to our work. I can't wait to show you the next stop on our journey."

I was excited to hear that.

The Irish in Michigan
Mackinac Island—August 1840

When we got back to the professor's office, he had to take a phone call.

"Yes, Sweetie Pie," said the professor. "Everything's just fine. No. No. Yes. He's just fine. Well, yes, I did have to give him a talking to about wandering off, but he is safe and doing well. We are having a wonderful time together. Alright, I will see you this evening. Goodbye."

"Was that your wife?" Rachel asked.

"Heaven's no," said Professor Tuesday, "that was Mister Adams's mother."

"But you called her Sweetie Pie," Owen said.

The professor looked confused. "I called her that because that's her name ... Sweetie Pie."

"So you are telling us that Mister Adams's mother is named 'Sweetie Pie'?" I asked.

"Why, yes," said the professor.

"Your family has some weird names, Professor," Owen said.

Professor Tuesday laughed out loud, "I guess we do at that."

Rachel played tic-tac-toe with Mister Adams while the professor prepared for our next visit into history. Mister Adams won every game. Rachel wasn't very happy about that. She likes to win. Owen was looking at a book about the Finns in Michigan. As he read the book, his lips moved with every word. That bugged Rachel, too.

Professor Tuesday's glasses slipped to the end of his nose. As he tapped away at his keyboard, he stopped for a moment, then he looked up. "Owen, Rachel, Jesse," he asked, "did you bring jackets?"

"My mother put a jacket in my backpack," Rachel said. "It's supposed to rain this afternoon."

Owen shuffled over to his backpack and started fishing around inside of it. "Yah, I've got one."

I showed the professor my jacket. "Why did you ask if we had jackets?"

"We'll be heading to northern Michigan, and it's usually colder there than it is here."

Professor Tuesday made one last keystroke, then hit the ENTER key on his laptop. The Tuesday Teleporter started its display of light and sound. Then the green cloud formed at the end of the professor's desk.

Before we stepped into the past, Professor Tuesday turned to his nephew. "Mister Adams, I talked to your mother a few minutes ago. She told me that if you are extra good this afternoon, she'll make you spinach for dinner."

Mister Adams got all excited. He started jumping up and down, clapping his hands.

"Euw-w-w-w," Rachel squealed, "spinach. I hate spinach. He loves peanut-butter-and-jelly and pickle sandwiches, and he actually likes spinach."

Professor Tuesday lifted his glasses slightly. "Spinach is very good for you. Mister Adams loves it. Spinach is a special treat for him."

"He can have my share," Owen said. "I don't like it either."

"We're going to visit some immigrants who left their homeland to come to Michigan because they were starving. They would have been happy to eat spinach, even if they didn't like it," said the professor. He adjusted our translators before we put them on our ears. "Put your jackets on before we go."

I felt sick to my stomach as I tumbled over and over through time. I thought to myself, "Maybe I shouldn't be doing this right after eating all that spaghetti." But, before long, we were standing on a beach. It didn't look like the sandy beaches I visit when my family goes on vacation up north. The edge of the water was dotted with big rocks for as far as I could see.

The wind coming off the water was very cold. My teeth began chattering. I was glad the professor told us to wear our jackets. Gulls drifted in the wind above us squawking loudly. Birds dove into the water for fish. Off in the distance, boats bobbed in the blue waves.

Professor Tuesday took a look at his compass and pointed down the shoreline. "Let's go this way," he said.

We picked our way through the rocks. Owen stopped now and then to skip stones on the water. Mister Adams seemed to enjoy watching him. The professor's nephew even tried to skip a stone himself. But it just went KERPLUNK into the icy cold water.

"What is it with boys?" Rachel asked to no one in particular. "Why do they always have to throw rocks?"

Owen didn't even bother answering Rachel. He just kept pitching rocks into the lake.

"Where are we, professor?" I asked.

Professor Tuesday stopped and turned to answer. "We are on Mackinac Island in 1840. I'd like to visit some Irish immigrants. You'll notice that there aren't any fudge shops, T-shirt stores, or high-powered ferry boats. But, the island has been a popular vacation spot even before 1840, just as it is in our time."

As we rounded a point on the island, a beautiful harbor stretched out ahead of us. We could see several boats pulled up on shore. Men were climbing in and out of the boats. They were working on something. Professor Tuesday stopped so we could watch.

The workers lifted heavy nets out of the boats. They pulled fish from the nets and threw them into large buckets on the shore. The air smelled like fish and pine trees. We turned away from the harbor and began walking up a road. Businesses and homes lined both sides of the street. A huge fort sat at the top of a big hill outside of town.

The professor was going to make a point about something when he looked around. His face told me that he was scared.

"Where's Mister Adams?" asked the professor.

"Where's Owen?" Rachel asked.

"The last time I saw them, they were skipping stones and throwing rocks into the lake. Maybe they fell into the water," I said.

Professor Tuesday ran back to where we began our journey on Mackinac Island. We looked high and low in and around the water. Owen and Mister Adams were nowhere to be found. We shouted their names, but no one called back.

It was time to start worrying again.

Finding Friends
Mackinac Island—August 1840

After we searched the area where the two of them had been, we headed back toward the harbor. As we passed some fishing boats, we saw them. They were standing near the shore next to one of the big buckets of fish.

Owen and Mister Adams looked up as we walked toward them. "Professor," Owen said excitedly, "did you see the size of these fish? They're huge! I've never caught one so big. Shucks, I've never even seen fish this big."

A fisherman walked up and threw more fish into the big bucket.

"Hey, mister," Owen called out to the man, "what kind of bait are you using?"

The man gave Owen a funny look and went back to his work.

Professor Tuesday was upset as he talked to the two of them. "Owen! Mister Adams! You scared us very badly. Please don't wander off like that. We didn't know if you fell in the lake or got lost on the island."

Mister Adams looked sad. Owen hung his head as he spoke softly, "Sorry, Professor, it's just that I got excited when I saw those big fish. I had to take a closer look. It's my fault, not Mister Adams's. I was the one who decided to come over here. We should have stayed by you, but I did watch him very carefully."

"Owen," Rachel said angrily, "you are always goofing up. When will you ever learn?"

"I understand your excitement," the professor said. "I'm just glad that you're safe. From now on, let's stay together at all times, no matter what. Oh, and the Irish fishermen here were using nets. They didn't use bait. Now, there's someone in town I want you to meet."

We walked up the shoreline and followed the road. Professor Tuesday walked into one of the buildings. Above the door was a sign that read "General Store."

"Are we going to buy something?" Rachel asked. "I need a new pair of flip-flops. My dad gave me some money."

The professor held the door open for us as we walked inside. "Our money and credit cards won't work in 1840. And, we don't have much to trade. Besides, they probably don't have anything you'd want."

Owen, Mister Adams, Rachel, and I walked around inside the store. The professor was right. They didn't have any of the cool stuff that I like to look at when I visit Mackinac Island. The store didn't even have a computer or a cash register. We only saw tools, some flour and food items, and a few clothes. Rachel and I weren't interested in the clothes that were in the store. They were the kind of things people wore in olden times. There weren't even any postcards, sand toys, or bobblehead dolls.

While we looked around, the professor talked to the man behind the counter. "Good day, sir," the professor said. His translator changed his words as he spoke. "Is it possible that I am talking to Mr. O'Malley, the owner of this fine establishment?"

The man puffed up his chest. "Why, yes," said the man, as he reached out his hand to the professor, "and you are?"

"My name is Tuesday," said the professor. "My friends and I have traveled afar just to meet you." Then the professor introduced each of us to Mr. O'Malley.

While we visited with Mr. O'Malley, he talked to us about his store and his hopes for a better life than he had in Ireland. After our chat, the professor reached into his coat pocket and took out two pencils. The professor handed the two pencils to Mr. O'Malley and showed him how the erasers worked.

"These are fine writing instruments," the professor said. "Would you trade them for a few pieces of hard candy for my young friends?"

Mr. O'Malley's eyes were wide with excitement. "Certainly," he said. Mr. O'Malley reached behind the counter and took out a glass jar. He took off the glass lid, and we each took a piece of candy.

"We must be going now," said the professor. "We have much to do yet today, but first we need to rest." He thanked Mr. O'Malley and we went outside.

Relaxing Near the Fort
Mackinac Island—August 1840

Owen, Rachel, and Mister Adams popped their hard candies into their mouths. I wanted to save mine, so I put it in my jacket pocket. Mister Adams smiled widely as he sucked on the sweet treat. Owen tried to chew on his piece, but it was too hard. Rachel just shook her head at him.

"Everyone knows that you don't chew hard candy," Rachel said. "Everyone except Owen, that is."

"Can you give it a rest?" Owen asked. "She-e-e-sh."

Seagulls swooped in and out above our heads as we walked along the road that led to the fort on the hill. We sat in the tall grass beneath a large tree. Professor Tuesday took off his shoes and socks once again, but no one else did. He leaned on one elbow as he rested in the grass. "Remember the first time your class came to see me? We talked about Pontiac's war of 1763. Well," the professor said, "this is the island that the native people called the 'great turtle.'"

"I remember," said Rachel.

"What did we learn about Irish immigrants on this trip?" the professor asked.

"There wasn't much to see," Owen said. His words sounded funny because he had a mouthful of candy. "Of course we saw some big fish and a store."

"Who was that O'Malley guy we met?" Rachel asked.

"We'll talk about Charles O'Malley a little later," said the professor. "What were the first things you saw on Mackinac Island?"

"We started out on a rocky beach," Owen said. He put his finger to the side of his head as he thought. "There were some fishing boats out on the water. It looked like they were catching a lot of fish. One time my dad and I caught thirty perch. But those guys back on the island were really catching fish, big ones and lots of 'em."

"Yes, they were," said the professor. "Many Irish immigrants in the mid-1800s became fishermen in Michigan. Several took up fishing on Mackinac Island, Beaver Island, and other islands and port cities around the state."

"So, the Irish were fishermen?" Owen asked. "I'd like that job. Fish are fun to catch. I use worms, but my dad likes to use minnows."

The professor scratched his head and blinked twice. "Fishing is only one of the jobs the Irish did.

Many of the Irish immigrants became fishermen here because they were professional fishermen in their home country. The Irish were also involved in farming, construction, and mining. If you recall our visit to the Erie Canal, many Irish immigrants worked to dig that canal and others. In fact, a few years after our visit to Mackinac Island, Irish workers helped to dig the canal at Sault Ste. Marie. This canal opened up all of the Great Lakes to shipping. The early railroads that crisscrossed the state were also built in large part by Irish workers."

"You said they were miners," Owen noted. "Did they work in the mines with the Finns?"

"Why, yes," said the professor. "I noticed that you were looking at books about the early Finns in Michigan. Good for you. Several immigrant groups, including the Irish and the Finns, worked in mining as well."

A big smile crossed the professor's face. "I just finished reading a magazine article about an Irishman named Billy Royal. According to the story, his pigs fell into a pit near Calumet, Michigan. Some claim that the pigs fell into a hole in the ground that was made by ancient copper miners. As the story goes, Billy Royal's pigs found the first evidence of a rich deposit of copper known as Calumet Conglomerate." Professor Tuesday winked twice at us. "Nobody knows if the story is true or not, but it is a good story, don't you think?"

I raised my hand to ask a question. "You talked about spinach before ... that reminds me of something. You said that the Irish were starving in their homeland?"

"Excellent," said Professor Tuesday. "Between 1799 and 1815 there was a series of wars fought between France and several European nations. They were called the Napoleonic Wars because the French were led by Napoleon Bonaparte, the famous military leader. Once these wars were over, much of the world fell into an economic depression. In those times many immigrants, including the Irish, came to America looking for a better life.

"To make matters worse, a potato famine struck Ireland around the middle of the 1800s," added the professor. "When their crops failed, starving Irish fled their country. They believed that coming to America was their best hope. Michigan proved to be a great place for many of them to settle. Just so you know, Michigan was, and still is, a great place for growing potatoes."

We were all quiet for a while, thinking about how terrible it would be to starve. I guess that if I were starving, I'd eat spinach ... but only if I had to.

Owen spoke up once again. "Like I said, the fishermen were catching a lot of fish, and big ones, too."

"The Great Lakes provided much of the food for early settlers in Michigan," the professor said. "It looked like the fishermen were catching lake trout. As you may know, Mackinac Island is on Lake Huron. In terms of water volume, Lake Huron is the third largest of the Great Lakes after Lake Superior and Lake Michigan."

"Professor," I said, "there's a big fort on the top of the hill. Can you tell us about it?"

"What you are looking at is Fort Mackinac as it was in 1840," said Professor Tuesday. "The fort itself was originally built by the British in 1780. It played a role in the French and Indian War and the War of 1812. When peace finally came to the frontier, traders like Charles O'Malley set up businesses on the island in the shadows of the fort."

"Can you tell us about Mr. O'Malley?" I asked.

The professor smiled as he put his hands on the back of his head. "I've always wanted to meet Charles O'Malley."

"Really?" I asked.

The professor nodded his head. "Mr. O'Malley immigrated to the state in 1835. He was originally from Dorrada, county Mayo, Ireland. O'Malley thought about being a priest, but when he came to Michigan he helped to build an Irish settlement on Mackinac Island. He also ran a very successful general store."

"So, we were in Mr. O'Malley's store?" I added.

"Correct," said Professor Tuesday, "but that's not the end of the story. Mr. O'Malley was also interested in politics. He held several offices on the island and served in the state legislature. He was first elected in 1846. His work in the legislature can still be seen around Michigan."

"How so?" Rachel asked.

"Well, he gave Irish names to several northern Michigan counties," said the professor. "County names such as Wexford, Antrim, Clare, and Emmet are all Irish names."

"How cool is that!" said Owen. "An immigrant moved from Ireland to Michigan in 1835. After only 11 years in this country, he gets elected to the state legislature."

"Mr. O'Malley has a very interesting place in Michigan history," said the professor. "I've always wanted to meet him, and your project on immigrants gave me the chance. So, thank you for that."

Professor Tuesday thought for a moment before continuing, "Did you notice anything else?"

"I noticed that they made pretty good candy back in the 1800s," Owen said. Mister Adams nodded his head in agreement and clapped his hands.

Professor Tuesday, Mister Adams, and I had a good laugh. Rachel didn't think what Owen said was all that funny.

"Well, Owen," the professor said, "you've been reading a little about the Finns. Where should we go to visit some of them?"

"We should go to the Keweenaw Peninsula," Owen said.

"Very good," said Professor Tuesday. "You paid close attention to your reading."

The professor put his shoes and socks back on, then stood up. He turned to his nephew, "Mister Adams, when we get back to my office, remind me to pack a bag of safety gear. We'll be heading into the deep wilderness."

For some reason, the idea of needing to take safety gear on our next trip was kind of scary to me.

Computer Conflict
The Professor's Office—Today

After we stepped through the teleporter, we found ourselves in the warmth of the professor's office once again. Mackinac Island had been chilly and windy.

"I have to check my phone messages and e-mail before we go anywhere else," the professor said as he turned to his desk and began working on his computer.

Rachel and Owen wrote in their journals as I watched the professor's nephew. Mister Adams and I played tic-tac-toe for a while, then we had several games of hangman. He won every game. That didn't bother me at all. After a while, he got bored with playing games, so he picked up a history book and started to read.

I stared out the window and watched children playing in the park across the street from the professor's office building. As I looked out the window, I thought about coming along with Rachel and Owen to see Professor Tuesday. It would have been great to spend the whole day running and playing with my other friends. But, I was having fun in another way. I was enjoying myself by learning new things. It had been a fun day with my friends and Professor Tuesday. I was eager to learn more. My thoughts were interrupted when the professor started shouting and jumping around.

"Yippee," shouted the professor as he did a little dance. "I just won a new camera online."

Owen perked up, "Really? That's cool, Professor. How did you win a camera?"

"I just got an e-mail that told me I won," answered the professor. "When I opened up the message, all I had to do was fill out some information. My new camera should be here next week."

"Professor, did you know the company or person who sent you the e-mail?" Owen asked.

"Well, no," the professor answered.

Owen looked concerned, "It's not a good idea to open e-mails and give personal information to strangers."

Rachel glared at Owen. "The professor knows what he's doing, mind your own business."

"Well," said the professor, "I'm excited about my new camera. It will be great to take along on my trips into the past."

"When are we taking our next trip?" I asked.

"Right now," answered the professor.

He turned to his computer and started working. As the professor input information into his laptop, he began to look a little concerned.

"Is everything alright?" Owen asked.

"My computer is acting up," said the professor. "If I can't get it to run right, we won't be able to visit Copper Country."

The professor picked up his laptop and shook it twice. Then he fiddled with some keys and let out a big sigh.

Rachel just stood back and didn't say anything ... for a change.

Owen asked the professor if he could take a look at his laptop. When the professor agreed, my friend took a seat at the professor's desk and started working on the computer. Mister Adams stood by Owen and watched him.

"What are you going to do?" asked the professor.

"Your computer locked up," Owen said. "I'm going to restart it and check it for system conflicts."

"What?" asked the professor.

Without looking up from the laptop, Owen explained, "I'm going to see if you have some programs on your computer that don't get along with each other."

"Just like you and me," Rachel said.

"A lot like you and me," Owen answered.

Owen tapped away at the keyboard as Professor Tuesday watched over his shoulder. Rachel and I played games with Mister Adams as we waited. Rachel was worried that Owen might ruin the professor's computer and that they'd never get their report done.

"There," said Owen, "that ought to do it." He turned to the professor as he shut down the computer. "I have to re-start your laptop to accept the changes I've made."

"Changes? You made changes to my computer?" the professor said as a worried look crossed his face.

"Don't worry, Professor," Owen said. "Your computer had some spyware that was creating problems. You may have picked it up from the e-mail that offered you a free camera. That's why you should be careful about the messages you open. I just removed the spyware, that's all. Once your laptop starts up again, it should run much better."

When the computer started again, it was running smoothly. "Thank goodness," the professor said as he wiped his brow. "I'll be more careful about the messages I open from now on."

"Well," Rachel noted, "it looks like Owen is good for something after all."

"Rachel," I said, "can't you say something nice for once?"

The professor went back to work, programming our next trip into his computer. When he hit the ENTER key to start up the Tuesday Teleporter, the globe lit up and colorful lights started circling the room once again. Around and around they went as the noises grew and grew. Slowly the green cloud took shape by the professor's desk. He peeked inside quickly.

"It's cold and raining in Houghton," he said. "Better put on your jackets."

As we were about to walk into the green cloud, Owen sneezed again, then tripped on his shoelaces. As my friend fell, he hit his head on the corner of Professor Tuesday's desk with a big THUNK. We had to stop and wait until he finished fixing his glasses. Then he rubbed the goose egg that was growing on his forehead.

"I don't think he'll ever learn," said Rachel.

Mister Adams looked at the bump on Owen's noggin. Then he signed two letters ... O and K.

"Thanks, Mister Adams," Owen said, "I'm okay."

I could tell that Owen was hurt, but he's pretty tough.

The Immigrants of Copper Country

Houghton, Michigan— September 1866

The professor was right. It was a cold and miserable day in Copper Country. We landed in a forest of tall pine trees. A thick layer of pine needles under our feet made it feel like we were walking on pillows. The professor pulled out his compass. We followed him as he started walking. All the while, the three of us kept close watch on Mister Adams to make sure he didn't wander off again.

A chilly wind blew off the lake and dark clouds covered the sky. There was steady drizzle coming down as we walked out of the woods and toward a muddy street. We could see water behind us and a large ship tied up at a dock. The ship had tall masts that looked like huge flagpoles poking into the sky.

Its sails were neatly folded up and tied. It reminded me of those tall ships that take people for rides in Traverse City. Sailors were working on the deck and high on the masts and rope lines. On shore, men were taking crates and barrels off the ship. Others were loading barrels back on board. It all looked like very hard work.

We came to a stop on the road. "This is Quincy Street," said the professor. Then he pointed up the hill, away from the water. "Right up ahead is the Quincy Mine. I think we should stop by and see what kind of work is going on there."

"This isn't much of a street," Rachel said. "It's more like one big mud puddle."

Owen and I agreed. What a mess! Our shoes and pants were covered in mud. The farther we walked, the muddier we got.

The professor stopped before we got to the mine. "Take a good look around," he said. "Think about what you see and take careful notes in your journals."

The big, dark lake behind us blended in with the cloudy sky. Once again there were tall, thick trees everywhere. Huge pines grew right to the lakeshore. They lined the muddy streets and stretched as far as we could see. The rain had scoured deep ruts in the sandy road.

Rachel wrote down descriptions of everything she saw. Owen mostly drew pictures.

The Quincy Mine
Houghton, Michigan— September 1866

We picked our way up the muddy street, jumping between puddles as best we could. They were everywhere. Owen and Mister Adams were trailing behind the professor, Rachel, and me. When I turned to look back at them, they were jumping in mud puddles and laughing out of control. When Mister Adams saw me looking at him, he put two fingers from his right hand by his nose while pointing outward with the two fingers of his left hand. Then he brought his right hand down.

I looked back to Professor Tuesday, and he was smiling. "Mister Adams says he's having fun. I think the two of them are becoming friends."

"I could be Mister Adams's friend if I wanted to," Rachel said. "But, I've already got a lot of friends."

"Oh," said the professor, "can a person have too many friends?"

Rachel didn't know how to answer the professor's question, so she just shrugged her shoulders.

Suddenly, something caught my eye. There was movement in the shadows of the forest. I thought it was a big dog, but I wasn't sure. I don't like big dogs. They scare me. Whatever it was, it seemed to be following us. When I tried to get a better look, it seemed to vanish. I didn't say anything to the professor. Maybe I should have. I was feeling a little nervous.

After walking about a block and a half, we started to come across several small wooden buildings. They looked very rough, more like broken-down shacks than houses. Thin wisps of smoke drifted out of the chimneys. I liked the smell of wood smoke. Now and then little children in tattered, dirty clothes could be seen running and playing in the rain. I shivered as I watched them.

At the end of the road we saw a large wooden building. Men were hauling wagons full of rocks toward the back. Others were hauling barrels of rocks out the front. The loads looked heavy as the men strained to push them along.

Suddenly, a noise came from behind us. We turned to see a group of workers coming toward us up the road. They were carrying picks, shovels, chisels, hammers, lanterns, and other tools. They passed us without a word and walked into a smaller building on the hillside. As they stepped into the building, others came out.

"Let's watch and see what happens," the professor said.

Those going into the building looked kind of clean and neat. The men coming out were covered in dirt and mud from head to toe. Their faces were black with grime. One by one they walked over to the side of the big building and washed up in water from a wooden barrel. Once most of the mud was cleaned off their hands and faces, they gathered underneath a tree and started eating their lunches. Their food looked like some kind of piecrust. Professor Tuesday came around and adjusted our Tuesday Translators so we could understand what they were saying.

The translators crackled in our ears as we listened. One man talked about finding a nice vein of copper. He told his friend that the copper was several inches thick and as long as his arm. The other man mentioned that he was working on a crew that found a big rock of native copper. The rock was so big that they couldn't get it out of the mine by hand. His crew was chiseling away at the boulder so they could take it out piece by piece.

"Professor," Owen asked, "can we go down into the mines? I'd sure like to see what it looks like."

"Heavens no," said the professor. "Mining is a dangerous business. Copper mines often cut deep into the hillsides. And, rats and bats like to make their homes in mines."

"E-w-w-w," Rachel squealed. "I hate bats, and I hate rats even more.

The professor continued, "The mines were dark, dirty, and wet. Miners often used wooden beams to keep the ceiling of the mine from caving in around them. Still, there were many, many accidents in the mines. The mining companies here in the Keweenaw tried to hire the best and most skilled workers. Some of these men came from Scandinavian countries, like Finland, Sweden, and Norway. Others came from mining areas such as Cornwall in England."

The professor thought for a time before continuing. "As you can see by looking at the men who just came out of the mine, it is a very dirty business. The miners often go deep into the earth to find veins of copper. They use heavy hammers and chisels to dig out what was called 'red metal.' Rocks and pieces of copper are carried to the surface, where it was sorted then shipped throughout the United States."

We sat quietly for a while and listened as the miners continued talking. The two of them talked about their families and children. Then one of them mentioned something that scared me.

"We must be very careful with our children," he said. "Isak told me he saw a wolf behind his house the other night."

"A wolf," the other man replied, "I thought that Johan chased the pack off for good."

"Well, I think they are back. Anyway, we must all watch the children and our animals very carefully."

I swallowed hard. Maybe I had seen the wolf in the shadows alongside the road. "Professor, can we go now?" I asked. "I'm getting cold."

Lost in Copper Country
Houghton, Michigan— September 1866

As we headed back I was careful to keep a close eye on Rachel, Owen, and Mister Adams. The idea of wolves nearby scared me. I didn't want anything to happen to me or anyone else.

Professor Tuesday stopped short and took a look at his watch. "Oh, my gosh, look what time it is." He held up his watch for us to see, but he put his arm down so fast we couldn't tell what time it was.

"We don't have time to discuss this visit right now," the professor said. "I want to see more before the day is over."

We headed back toward the spot where the teleporter dropped us off. As we approached the pine forest, a cloud of insects greeted us.

"Oh, no," said the professor, "Keweenaw eagles."

"Eagles ... where?" Owen asked as he swatted insects away.

"Black flies," said the professor. "The miners called black flies 'Keweenaw eagles' because they were so big."

Professor Tuesday dug into his emergency pack and pulled out a can of insect repellant. We closed our eyes and plugged our noses as the professor sprayed us down. "Black flies and mosquitoes were another nasty hazard that immigrants in Copper Country faced."

We continued walking into the pine forest. It seemed like we had been walking a long time when the professor stopped and raised his hand.

"What's wrong, Professor?" Rachel asked.

"The teleporter cloud should be here somewhere," he said as worry crossed his face.

"Where is it?" Owen asked.

"I don't know," said the professor as he checked his compass.

"What do we do now?" I asked.

"The first thing we should do is to relax and not panic," said the professor. "I'm sure the teleporter is nearby. I want the three of you to stay here while I go look for it."

"Professor," I said, "maybe I should have said something before, but I thought I saw a wolf following us. I don't know, maybe it was just a big dog ... maybe."

"Oh, no!" Rachel cried. "I don't like big dogs or wolves."

Mister Adams gave her a big hug, and she settled down a bit, but we were all starting to get scared.

"It will be okay," said the professor. "I won't be far. I'll start a small fire. That should warm you up a bit. Plus, it will help to keep animals and bugs away." The professor turned to Owen. "Can you tend the fire safely?"

"I can, Professor," Owen said proudly. "And, we'll all take good care of Mister Adams."

The professor took some dry pine needles that were under the trees and protected from the rain. He quickly gathered up some twigs and small branches. Then he opened up his emergency pack and took out some matches. A small fire quickly came to life.

Before leaving, the professor turned to his nephew. "Mister Adams, it is very important that you stay with your friends and not wander."

Mister Adams gave the yes sign. Then the professor started off to search for the teleporter.

We huddled around the small fire and warmed our hands. Rachel started sniffling. It was easy to see that she was upset. The rain picked up a bit and the thick smoke got in our eyes. Owen watched the fire carefully. Now and then, he would gather up dead wood and throw it on the fire to keep it going. On one of his trips for firewood, Owen found a long sturdy branch that looked like a club.

"Don't worry," Owen said when he returned to the fire. "The professor will find the teleporter soon.

And, I've got this piece of wood I can use if a wolf comes around."

"Yah, right," Rachel said.

Suddenly, we heard something crashing through the forest. Whatever it was, it was close and seemed to be heading toward us. Rachel, Mister Adams, and I huddled together. Owen picked up his club and bravely headed toward the sound. When he thought he was close, Owen got himself ready to strike.

"It's me," said the professor, "I found the teleporter." He stepped out from behind some tall brush. It was just over the next hill. I don't know how I missed it, but we're safe now."

Owen ran to the professor's side. "Am I ever glad to see you. For a minute there, I thought there was a wolf coming after us."

The professor roughed up Owen's hair. "I'm pleased that I left you in charge of the fire," Professor Tuesday said. "You kept everyone safe, and I found my way back by following the smoke."

Our spirits rose as we put out the fire and headed toward the teleporter. It was a close call. Little did we know that something really scary was about to happen.

A Close Call
The Professor's Office—Today

When we got to the top of the hill, we were all excited to see the teleporter again.

Owen decided to keep his club as a souvenir of his trip to Copper Country. He held it in both hands as he followed the professor, Mister Adams, Rachel, and me into the teleporter cloud.

We all realized something was wrong once we landed back in the professor's office. A loud, low growling sound sent chills up and down my spine. We didn't see it at first. Finally, we saw two eyes glowing in the dark corner on the far side of the room. Slowly, steadily, a wolf edged into the light, baring its teeth. Rachel and I screamed. We grabbed Mister Adams and ran behind the professor's desk.

Owen stepped forward with his club and started swinging it back and forth. The club made whooshing sounds as it cut through the air. The wolf backed into the corner and continued its fierce growl.

"Professor, the wolf must have come through the teleporter," Owen whispered. "We've got to do something fast!"

"My goodness! My goodness!" the professor said. He joined Rachel, Mister Adams, and me behind his desk. "I'll re-set the teleporter to send it somewhere back in time. We've got to get that wolf out of here now. Does anyone have an idea of how we can do it?"

Rachel and I were too scared to think. "Don't let the wolf get us," Rachel cried.

Our eyes widened as Owen bravely swung his club back and forth. The wolf tried to come forward, but Owen managed to keep him cornered. The professor quickly tapped away at his laptop. While the professor worked, Mister Adams was rummaging through the drawers in his uncle's desk.

"Hurry, Professor!" Owen shouted over his shoulder. "I can't hold it off much longer."

I looked over at the professor and saw Mister Adams open a cheese stick. At first I thought it was a funny time to look for something to eat. Then I understood what he was doing. Mister Adams threw the cheese stick to the wolf. The animal stopped growling and quickly gobbled up the treat.

"Keep throwing treats to the wolf," shouted the professor. "I'm almost done here."

Another cheese stick flew through the air and landed near the dark corner. It, too, was quickly snapped up by the wolf. Rachel and I crept closer to the professor as the wolf continued growling and baring its big teeth.

"Done," shouted the professor as a green cloud once again appeared in his office. Mister Adams took a cheese stick and threw it into the cloud. The wolf chased the food and disappeared into the past. Professor Tuesday quickly closed the teleporter and sat down hard in his chair.

"Whew, that was close," the professor said with a sigh. "Owen, you are a hero."

Owen put his club down and started shaking. Mister Adams and I ran to his side. "You did a great job, Owen," I said. "Don't you agree, Rachel?"

"I suppose," Rachel said, "but now that we're all safe, I'd like to learn more about immigrants in Michigan."

"Rachel," I said, "you are a royal pain."

"We can continue our research if we can do it safely," said the professor. "I don't need another scare like we had with that wolf. My old heart can't take it. But this should be a good lesson to all of us. Immigrants who came to early Michigan had to face many dangers, including wild animals."

Professor Tuesday's hands shook as he picked up a book from his desk. He scratched his noggin as he paged through it. "Yes, yes," said the professor to no one in particular, "we probably should take a look at that."

"Take a look at what?" Owen asked. Mister Adams shook his head. He was curious, too.

"I want to visit an early lumber camp," said the professor. "But the lumber companies mostly operated during the winter." Professor Tuesday shrugged his shoulders twice. "We don't have warm coats, and I don't want anyone to catch cold by visiting the north woods at that time of the year. Plus, there were wolves, bears, and coyotes roaming the woods in those days."

You could tell by the look in Mister Adams's eyes that he was thinking. Suddenly, he pointed one finger in the air to get Professor Tuesday's attention. Then he started spelling out words in sign language.

"Slow down, Mister Adams," the professor said, "I can't understand what you are signing when you go so fast."

Mister Adams scowled at the professor and started all over again. The professor wrote down each letter on a piece of paper. When Mister Adams was done, the professor read aloud, "Peek inside the cloud."

"Silly me," said the professor, "Mister Adams is right. We can set up the teleporter and just peek inside. When our heads get too cold, we'll just pull them back. What a great idea! Mister Adams," the professor said proudly, "you are a genius."

Mister Adams agreed and nodded his head.

A Peek into the Lumbering Era
Near Oscoda, Michigan— January and May 1850

Professor Tuesday plinked away at his keyboard as Owen and Rachel looked through the notes they'd taken so far. Rachel is a better note keeper than Owen, but he's better at drawing. While they looked through their journals, Mister Adams began to play with a Rubik's Cube. I've got one at home, but I've never been able to solve it. Mister Adams solved it in less than a minute.

"How'd he do that so fast?" Rachel asked.

I just shrugged my shoulders. "Maybe he's a genius."

As I was watching Mister Adams, the professor called out, "Let's take a look into the lumbering era in the mid-1800s."

We gathered around as Professor Tuesday hit the ENTER key on his laptop one more time. After the lights and sounds settled, the green cloud formed at the corner of his desk. We all poked our heads into the green cloud.

What a funny feeling! Our heads rattled around in time for a moment, then settled in a forest area in the middle of winter. It looked like northern Michigan, but I couldn't tell just where. Our heads were very cold, but the rest of our bodies stayed warm in the professor's office. I thought about what it would be like to be discovered by some lumberjacks. It made me laugh to think that seeing heads floating in a green cloud would make a good camp story.

We were near a camp in the deep woods. A shabby looking wooden bunkhouse was at the far side. A smaller building stood near it. By the smells that came from the smaller building, I guessed it was the kitchen or something. The sounds of ringing metal came from still another shed. A barn or stable was standing at the far end of the camp. Horses and oxen were feeding in the corral next to it.

The sound of voices carried through the woods. The Tuesday Translator in my ear clicked and clacked as it tried to keep up with the different languages that were being spoken. One man standing by the bunkhouse spoke in broken English as he pointed to a stand of pine trees. Two men hustled over to the nearest tree.

Though it was very cold, the men only wore light jackets. Their pants were tucked into tall boots. Floppy hats were pulled down tightly on their heads.

One of them smoked a pipe. They both had scraggly beards.

As we continued to look around the camp, our attention was captured by loud chopping sounds. The two men stood on opposite sides of a tall pine tree. They took turns swinging heavy axes. Each swing of the axe bit deep into the tree. I wondered how long it would take these guys to chop one down. My head was getting cold.

A man was leading a horse and sled down an ice-covered trail. When the sled passed us, I could see water sprinkling out of a tank on the back. I guessed the icy road would be used for hauling logs.

"Let's pull our heads back and get warmed up," said the professor. His breath was frosty when he spoke.

When we came out of the green cloud, I put my hands over my ears to warm them up.

"Whew," said Owen, "my nose was freezing."

The professor stepped behind his desk and typed in some new information on his laptop. "While we warm ourselves I'm going to change our location and time a little bit. We'll be a mile or so from the camp and in the early spring of the year. I want to show you how the shanty boys got trees to the sawmill."

"What's a shanty boy?" Rachel asked.

"Shanty boy is another term for logger or lumberjack," answered the professor.

Once our ears and noses warmed up, we took a second peek into the past. Like the professor said, we were in a different place and at a different time. It was still cold, but it was not as cold as before.

We were near a high bank that ran alongside a river. Huge logs were in neat, tall stacks on the bank. A man walked carefully among the stacks of logs. Then he took what looked like a hammer and struck each log soundly before moving on to the next pile of timber.

While the man with the hammer kept at his task, other men and animals worked together to roll the logs to the edge of the bank. Long poles and horses pushed the logs over the edge. They rolled down the steep bank and splashed into the river below. In the river, there were men standing on the floating logs. They were separating the logs with long poles that had hooks and points on the end. I wondered how they could possibly keep their balance on those logs in a moving river.

As logs were rolled down the bank, more were being delivered. Large loads of logs chained to sleds were being pulled by teams of horses along one of the ice roads. While we watched, a horn blared in the distance. When the men heard it, they stopped their work and started running in the direction of the sound. I wondered what was going on.

The professor made a sign that it was time to go.

Copper Country Chat
The Professor's Office—Today

The professor made himself some tea and poured some milk for us. Then he opened a bag of cookies. Yum!

Professor Tuesday smacked his lips as he nibbled on a cookie and sipped his tea. "Lumbering and mining in the state of Michigan drew thousands of immigrants looking for work. Many came thinking they would make their fortune and then use the money to buy their own farm or start a business." Professor Tuesday looked at Owen and me. "What did you think of Houghton, Michigan?"

"It was cold, rainy, and muddy," Rachel said. "The mine looked dirty and dangerous. I didn't like going there at all."

Mister Adams cupped his hands in front of himself and moved them forward.

"You were paying attention," said the professor. "Mister Adams said that he saw a boat."

"It was a tall ship," Owen said. "You know, with sails and stuff. I've seen them before, when my family visited Traverse City and Bay City."

"Yes," replied the professor. "Though there were many steamships operating on the Great Lakes in 1866, cargo and passengers were still carried by sailing ships. It looked like they were taking food and supplies off the ship and loading barrels of copper onto it. On May 31, 1855, the Soo Locks and the canal around the St. Mary's Rapids were completed. This opened up Lake Superior and the Upper Peninsula to greater trade. At the same time, it allowed immigrants, like miners and lumberjacks, easier travels to that part of the state."

The professor turned to Owen. "What was our purpose for visiting Houghton, Michigan, and a lumber camp near Oscoda, Michigan?"

"To see some Finnish immigrants," Owen answered.

"That's true," said the professor, "but I also wanted to show you how the availability of jobs in Michigan drew immigrants from many countries. In June of 1865, about thirty Finns arrived by boat at Houghton, Michigan, in the Keweenaw Peninsula. Many of the men who had worked at the mine up until that time had gone off to fight in the American Civil War, so the mine needed help."

"Professor, I'm just curious. When was copper discovered in the Upper Peninsula in the first place?" Owen asked.

"Native Americans first found copper there thousands of years ago," answered Professor Tuesday. "They used it to make tools, pots, and other things. In 1841, a state geologist named Douglass Houghton visited the area to investigate rumors that there was copper in the Keweenaw Peninsula. A year later, the native Chippewa people sold their rights to 25,000 square miles west of Marquette, Michigan, under the Treaty of La Pointe. Houghton's findings and the availability of this land led to a rush of prospectors, miners, and settlers.

"One of the favorite ways early prospectors used for finding copper was to look for old pits that had been dug by native people. One man, named Sam Knapp, stumbled on a large clearing in the forest in 1848. When he dug through the snow, Sam found the opening of a man-made cave. He and his friends explored the cave and found stone hammers and ancient mining tools. In the center of the cave was a huge nugget of copper. Sam Knapp's discovery of that old copper mine resulted in one of the most profitable copper mines in history. It was called the Minesota Mine. Somehow, a clerk spelled the word *Minnesota* wrong. That's how the mine got its funny spelling."

"There was one particular piece of copper that the native people found long before the Europeans came to Michigan," added the professor. "It came to be called the Ontonagon Boulder because it was found on the Ontonagon River. It weighed about 3,000 pounds. Today what is left of that boulder is kept at the Smithsonian Museum in Washington, D.C."

"So, Finns were the miners in Copper Country," Owen said.

"The Finns were just some of the many people who worked in the copper mines," said Professor Tuesday. "Finns, Swedes, Danes, Germans, Irish, Cornish, and others came to the North Country. They all had to learn to work together, overcome their differences, and get along. The same was true in the lumber camps of Michigan."

Talking Timber
The Professor's Office—Today

The professor took another sip of tea before continuing, "What do you remember from the lumber camp visit?"

"We saw some buildings. They didn't look like they were very well built," I said.

The professor nodded. "The buildings used in the lumber camps were made to be put up and taken down quickly. They would build a camp near where the trees were being cut. When all the trees near the camp were cut, the buildings would be taken down and re-built in the next cutting area."

"Did you smell the cookhouse?" asked the professor. We all nodded our heads. "I love the smell of bacon and pancakes. I have two pancakes for dinner every Tuesday."

"Just a minute, I've got a food question about Copper Country," Rachel said. "What was that pie that the miners were eating for lunch?"

"Oh, that was a pasty," said the professor. "It's a Cornish food that looks like a piecrust stuffed with meat, potato, rutabaga, and onion. Pasties were a favorite food of miners and lumberjacks because it was easy to carry and eat … even in a mine. Now, let's talk more about the lumber camp.

"I saw a stable," Owen said.

"Very good," replied the professor. "Horses and oxen were important work animals in the lumber camps and the mines. Animals were treated very well because they needed them to stay healthy and strong."

"It seemed like I heard a lot of different languages in both places," Owen said.

"Excellent," said the professor. "It sounded to me like the foreman in the lumber camp, the man shouting orders, was German. He was speaking English, but not very well. The men cutting down the pine tree were French-Canadian, I think."

"My father can speak three different languages," Rachel said.

The professor continued, "Sometimes, communicating was difficult in the camps due to all the different languages. But they learned to get along and work as teams. Communication between the workers was important because logging and copper mining are so very dangerous."

"What was that guy doing with the horse and the sleigh with a sprinkler?" I asked.

"He was building up the ice road," said the professor. "When the shanty boys would cut down trees, they would cut the tree trunk into lengths that would be easy to work with at the mills. The shanty boys would load the logs onto sleds, and teams of horses or oxen would pull the heavy loads over the ice road to a nearby river."

"So, that's why they worked in the winter months," I said. "That way they could build the ice roads making it easier to haul the logs. That was very smart. But, why did they cut down trees with axes? Wouldn't it have been easier to use saws to cut down trees?"

"Yes, it would have been easier and faster," said the professor. "But saws that cut down trees, called felling saws, weren't available until many years later. Now let's talk about what you saw on our second trip."

"I think it was later in the winter or early spring," Owen said. "The river down in the valley wasn't frozen over."

"I saw guys rolling logs down the hill. When the logs got to the bottom they rolled right into the river," Rachel added.

"Shanty boys who broke the piles of logs and sent them rolling down the banks into the river were called 'roll camp boys.'" The professor looked very excited. "The place you saw was called a 'rollaway.' It is located on the Au Sable River near what you may know as Oscoda, Michigan. Throughout the winter months, the shanty boys would cut down trees. Other workers would haul the logs to the rollaway and stack them up until spring. When the ice on the rivers and lakes started to melt away, roll camp boys would send the logs down to the river. This type of logging was called 'river logging' because the river was needed to move the logs to the mills."

"What was that guy doing with the hammer?" Owen asked. "Was he just whacking each log for luck or something?"

"Good question," said the professor. "He was marking the logs. Each lumber company had its own mark. It was sort of like a brand. Marks were used to identify who owned which logs."

"Who were those dudes on the river?" I asked. "It looked like they were standing on floating logs in the river. That's crazy. And, what were those poles they were carrying?"

The professor stroked his long beard. "The men on the river were called 'river hogs.' Being a river hog was dangerous, and only the toughest men in camp would ride the logs. River hogs rode the logs from the rollaway down river all the way to the sawmills. Their job was to prevent log jams. They used the poles to keep the logs moving downriver and for balance. Sometimes the log jams were so stubborn the river hogs couldn't break them. When that happened, they would use dynamite to blow up the log jam and get the logs moving again."

"Holy cow," Owen said, "I wish I could have seen that. I'll bet some of those logs blew sky high."

"They sure did," added the professor. "Then when the logs finally arrived at the sawmill they were cut into boards."

The professor blinked twice before continuing. "The lumber would be stacked and allowed to dry in the sun. When the boards were dry enough, they would be shipped across the Great Lakes to waiting customers."

The professor looked at each of us. "After all the work was done for the season, the lumber companies got paid. And, that's when they paid the shanty boys."

"What" I said, "they didn't get paid until the end of the season? That's lame."

"When they finally did get paid," the professor said, "they whooped it up in town." The professor looked at his watch again. "It's getting late, and there is one more place I want you to see before you go home."

Poletown

Hamtramck, Michigan—May 1882

The professor rushed to input information for our next trip while Owen and I played a game of catch with Mister Adams.

"Why are you just sitting there playing a game?" Rachel asked Owen. "We should be talking about our report, not goofing around. I get all *A*s on my report card, you get *B*s and *C*s. We have to work together on the immigration report, and I don't want you to mess up my grade."

"Get real," Owen said as he continued playing with Mister Adams.

While Owen was playing catch with Mister Adams, Rachel took a peek into his journal. The pages were nasty and wrinkled, not neat and clean like hers. Rachel kept careful notes about what she did and saw. Owen scratched a few notes down and drew pictures. Rachel was getting more and more upset.

Professor Tuesday adjusted the Tuesday Translators one more time before he spoke to us. "We have been very lucky so far," he said. "No one has been badly hurt or lost." He looked at Owen and Mister Adams. "We don't want anyone to wander off or get hurt, now do we?"

Owen and Mister Adams shook their heads no. Then the professor went to his laptop one last time. He hit the ENTER key and the teleporter popped to life. The globe rattled and hummed. Lights circled the room, and sounds thumped on the air. No matter how many times I've been through the teleporter, it is always an exciting adventure.

We stepped through the green cloud and landed safely in an alleyway. The alley was nothing more than a narrow dirt road carved with deep ruts. Dust clouded up around our ankles as we walked. Off in the distance, we could hear pounding.

"Be careful where you step," said the professor. "Horses, cows, and other animals are kept in these alleys."

"Yuk," Rachel said. "I wore my good school clothes and my best shoes. Oh well, they're already messy from our trip to Houghton."

A goose ran out into the alley from behind a small building. Rachel and I screamed and ran to the professor's side. A woman with a broom chased the goose. She wore a tattered old dress and a scarf on her head. Every time she got close to the goose, it would turn and run in a different direction. It honked loudly as it ran.

The Tuesday Translator crackled in my ear as she yelled at the goose. "You bad goose, get back to your own yard or we'll have you for dinner tonight."

We all laughed quietly at the funny sight. Then we continued on past small buildings. The air smelled like those animal barns at the fair. Some of the buildings had cows. Some had horses. We even saw a pig and a duck.

"Come this way," said Professor Tuesday. "I want you to see this."

Rachel and I picked our way carefully through the alley as we followed the professor. We ended up at a house that was being built. The wood that made up the walls was all in place. It looked like a house skeleton. There were about three rooms to the simple house. Men were sitting on narrow boards building the roof. They were calling out for nails and lumber. Every now and then, a man would tell a silly joke and all the others would laugh loudly.

As the professor, Mister Adams, and Owen were watching the house being built, Rachel and I noticed a girl staring at us from the alley behind us. She looked to be about eleven or twelve years old, but it was hard to tell. Rachel and I decided to talk with her. Maybe it would be helpful in Rachel's report.

She was very shy. As we got near, she looked down at her feet. The girl wore a scarf on her head just like the old woman we saw before. Her dress was clean and simple but very old looking. Worn shoes covered her small feet.

"My name is Rachel," my friend said.

"And I am Jesse," I said to the girl. "What is your name?"

"Sophia," she said. "You are not from here. You look very different."

"That is correct," Rachel said. The Polish words that came from the Tuesday Translator sounded funny in my ears. "We are far from home."

Sophia looked me over carefully. Then I spoke again, "What do you do each day?"

"I have much work to do," Sophia replied.

"Me, too," Rachel said. "My mother makes me clean my room and feed our dog every day. Plus, I have homework to do for school."

"I must help at home," Sophia said, "but I also have a job."

"A job?" I asked. "What kind of job?"

"I clean a doctor's house," Sophia said as she drew a circle in the dirt with her foot. "I must sweep, dust, and do dishes each day. Of course I also have to make all the beds and watch their small children. I only work six days a week." She added, "And, the doctor is very generous. He pays me $1.50 every Saturday."

"You do all that work for $1.50 a week?" Rachel asked.

"Yes, I am very lucky," Sophia said. "My wages help my family. The doctor also lets me eat food from his house."

I couldn't believe that a young girl would have a job like that. "If you have a job and work to do at home, when do you have time for school?"

"I have been to school," Sophia said. "After I graduated from the third grade, it was time for me to get a job and help my family. Don't you have a job?"

I shook my head no. "I just do some chores at home and go to school."

Sophia smiled at us. "It has been nice talking with you Rachel, and you, too, Jesse. I have to go now. It is a very long walk to my job, and I must not be late."

"It was nice talking with you, Sophia." My mind was spinning. Not only did she quit school in the third grade to take a job, but she has to walk to and from work each day. We watched Sophia as she went into her house. Things were really different back then.

We turned down the alleyway again to catch up with the professor, but when we looked up we gasped. The professor, Mister Adams, and Owen were nowhere to be seen. We were in big trouble.

Rachel and Jesse in Trouble
Hamtramck, Michigan—May 1882

"Professor ... Owen ... Mister Adams!" Rachel yelled, but there was no answer. Rachel and I ran down the alley to the place where the house was being built. None of our friends were there. Owen's sneakers left some prints in the dirty ruts. They seemed to be heading through a field away from the alley.

We were both getting scared and headed off into the field of tall weeds and wild flowers. Suddenly, Rachel started screaming.

"A bee ... a bee!" Rachel yelled at the top of her lungs. She swung her arms wildly at the insect that hovered above her head. "There are bees chasing me. I hate bees."

From across the field, I could hear the professor's voice. "Rachel, don't run, be still."

Rachel didn't pay any attention to the professor's advice. She kept running in circles and swinging her arms until she slipped and fell. I ran over to her and noticed that she was sitting in something that smelled very, very bad. The professor reached out with his hand to help her up.

"Rachel, Jesse," said the professor, "I am very disappointed in you. Before leaving my office, didn't we talk about not wandering off?"

"Y-Y-Yes, professor," Rachel stammered, "but I was talking with ..."

"It doesn't matter who you were talking with," said the professor.

"They're both sorry, professor," Owen said. "I'm sure it was just a mistake. It won't ever happen again."

Rachel spoke up, "It's not my fault all this happened. And look at me, my good shoes and school clothes are a mess."

"What stinks?" Owen asked.

Owen looked at the back of Rachel's school clothes. "Rachel," he said, "the field you just ran through is used as a cow pasture by all the families in this neighborhood. That wasn't mud that made you fall. I think you slipped and fell on some cow poop."

"Cow WHAT? ... Euw-w-w-w-w!"

Mister Adams pinched his nose and laughed.

When we returned through the Tuesday Teleporter, the professor told us to stay in his office. He went to the university bookstore to buy something for Rachel to wear. She couldn't stay in stinky clothes for the rest of the day.

"Owen," Rachel said, "thank you for standing up for Jesse and me with the professor. I feel awful."

"That's alright, Rachel," Owen said. "But why do you feel awful? Once you get cleaned up and put on some new clothes, you'll be fine."

"I know that," Rachel said. "I feel awful about the way I've been treating you."

Mister Adams shook his head in agreement.

"What do you mean?" Owen asked.

"When you trip or make some kind of mistake, I'm not very nice to you," Rachel said. "In fact, I usually say something mean. But, when I fell, you were kind to me. You even tried to help me. I've never tried to help you. I've never been nice to you." Rachel swallowed hard, "I'm sorry, I want to apologize for being so mean."

"That's alright, Rachel," Owen said. "I accept your apology. Now, let's find you a place to get cleaned up before the professor gets back."

Mister Adams pointed to the ladies' bathroom. It was just down the hall from the professor's office.

Owen and I stood outside the door with Mister Adams. I worked on a crossword puzzle while they bounced a ball against the wall in the hallway until the professor returned.

Before long the professor came back with a bag of clothes. "Rachel," called the professor from the hallway, "they didn't have much to choose from at the bookstore. So, I bought you a sweat suit. I'll throw it into the bathroom. You can get it once I close the door."

The bag flew into the bathroom and Rachel gathered it up in her arms. The sweatpants were just her size. The sweatshirt was a little too big, but that was fine. She likes them sloppy. The professor even thought to get her a pair of sneakers. They were a little big, too, but they'd work. Rachel picked up her dirty clothes and shoes and put them in the bag from the bookstore. When she got back to the professor's office, everyone was sitting around the professor's table.

"There she is," said the professor. "Come and join us. Do you feel better now that you've changed?"

"Yes, Professor, thank you for the clothes," Rachel answered. "It feels great to be clean again."

"You are welcome," he answered. "Now, let's talk about our visit to Hamtramck Township."

"Wait," Rachel said, "I want to tell you that I'm very sorry about not paying attention. I realize that I was wrong."

"I'm sorry, too, Professor," I added.

Professor Tuesday said, "That's all in the past now."

Mister Adams laughed so hard that he fell off his chair. Owen and the professor chuckled out loud. Then I got the joke and started laughing, too.

"What's so funny?" Rachel asked.

"The professor said, 'That's all in the past.' Get it? It's a joke," Owen said as he covered his smile.

Talk about Hamtramck
The Professor's Office—Today

"Let's get back to work," said the professor. "The place we visited was Hamtramck Township in 1882. The village of Hamtramck we know of today wasn't established until 1901. Long before Polish immigrants first came here to live, German and Irish immigrants farmed the land in the area."

"Where did they go?" Owen asked.

"Many immigrants who came to Michigan only settled in one place for a short time. Sometimes they would find better land for farming or a job in a different town. Other times they would move to a nearby area in the frontier. Some even moved as far as California."

The room went quiet until the professor spoke again. "Let's start from the beginning. What did you see during this trip?"

Owen was the first to speak. "We started out in an alley, I think. There were deep ruts in the dirt and garages on each side. So, the roads weren't much different from what they'd been like in 1837."

"Correct, but the buildings you saw weren't garages" said the professor. "They were barns. The Polish immigrants usually kept gardens in their yards plus horses, pigs, chickens, geese, and other animals in small barns behind their houses. For that matter, many other people across Michigan had barns in their backyards in those days."

"They also kept cows," Rachel said. "I found that out the hard way. And, that goose scared me, too."

"Yes, they did have cows," said the professor. A slight smile crossed his face. "Cows were particularly useful because of the milk they gave. Think about the Finns for a moment. When Lake Superior froze in winter, there was almost no way for the people of Copper Country to get supplies. So they had to rely on the food they stored and the animals they kept to help them survive."

"Why was that woman chasing the goose?" Owen asked.

"I don't know for sure," replied the professor as he combed his beard with his fingers. "Maybe it got away and she wanted it back in her yard."

"Why was that old lady wearing a scarf on her head?" Rachel asked. "Come to think of it, the girl we met, Sophia, also wore one."

"They were wearing babushkas," said the professor. "A babushka is a square piece of cloth that's folded into a triangle. It is a traditional Russian and Polish headscarf that is tied under the chin. The word *babushka* means 'old woman.'"

We all nodded our heads.

"Did you notice how small the houses were and how close all the houses were to each other?" asked the professor. "Why do you think they were built that way?"

Owen, Rachel, and I shrugged our shoulders. Mister Adams rolled his fingers together.

"That's right, Mister Adams," said the professor. "The Polish immigrants were trying to save money. Their property and houses were small and very inexpensive."

"Who do you think was building that house?" I asked.

"The immigrants themselves built most of their own homes," said Professor Tuesday. The professor blinked twice before continuing. "Polish immigrants, like many other immigrants to Michigan, practiced chain migration."

"What's chain migration?" Owen asked.

"Well," the professor started, "a few families would move to a certain place. Once they found work and a place to live, they would write to their relatives back in their home country. Often, they would send money to help their families migrate to Michigan. When the time was right and enough money was saved, a relative or another family in the home country might immigrate and move in with the family that was here. When the new immigrant family got work and saved enough money, they would build their own home. Usually, family and friends helped. That's how chain migration worked."

"What were you looking at while we were visiting with Sophia in the alley?" I asked.

"We'll talk about that in a minute, but I'm curious what you learned by talking to your friend Sophia," the professor replied. "Let's have a snack and talk about everything we saw."

Snacking on Immigration History
The Professor's Office—Today

Mister Adams picked up his Rubik's Cube and began fiddling with it as Owen and I worked on our journal entries. Professor Tuesday went to a small kitchen on the first floor of his building. He grabbed some fruit and yogurt from the refrigerator and brought them back for us to share.

When he returned to his office, the professor put down the tray of snacks and snapped his fingers twice. "There are some things I forgot to tell you about the Polish immigrants in Michigan."

"Like what?" Owen asked as he peeled a banana.

"First off," said the professor, "the earliest Polish immigrants in Michigan did not settle in what we now know as Hamtramck. One Polish settlement

149

was in Parisville, Michigan, near Port Huron. Muskegon also saw some early Polish immigrants as did the city of Calumet in the Keweenaw Peninsula."

"In Copper Country?" I asked.

"Yes," answered Professor Tuesday. "Others settled in the Grand Rapids area and different places around the state." Professor Tuesday rolled his eyes as he thought. "The other thing you should know is that many Polish immigrants who came to Michigan did not come directly from what we now call 'Poland.'"

"So, where did they come from?" Owen asked.

"Many of them came here from other states. Many Poles worked in coal mines from Pennsylvania to Ohio. Others worked on the railroads and other jobs in different states before they moved to Michigan. Poles were considered good, skilled workers. When Henry Ford built his automobile manufacturing business in Michigan, he preferred to hire Polish employees."

"What made Polish people want to come here?" Owen asked as he played with his ball cap.

"Land was cheap," the professor began, "plus Michigan offered plenty of opportunity for people who wanted to work."

"You just won't believe it," Rachel blurted out in excitement. "Sophia, the girl we were talking to, was just a kid like Owen, Jesse, and me, but she told me that she had a real job."

"Is that so?" asked the professor. "What kind of job did she have?"

"She was a maid or something," Rachel answered. "Sophia cleaned some doctor's house every day of the week except Sunday. She had to make the beds, do dishes, take care of the kids, and other stuff."

"That was not unusual," the professor said. "Back then, children often had jobs. Some children as young as seven years old took jobs. Many of them even had dangerous jobs—from coal mining to manufacturing. Shanty boys were often as young as fifteen." The professor scratched his chin as he continued, "In one of my books, I read that somewhere around 2 million children had jobs in 1810. Some of them worked as much as sixteen hours a day, six days a week. The children who worked in those days came mostly from poor families that needed the money."

"Whoa," said Owen. "I'm glad I didn't live back then."

"Did she tell you how much she was paid?" the professor asked.

"That's the other strange thing," Rachel answered. "She only got $1.50 for a whole week's work. That can't be true, can it, Professor?"

"Unfortunately, it probably is true," replied the professor. "Back then children were a cheap form of labor, that's why so many of them worked. And, each dollar back then was worth much more than it is in our time."

"Gee, that's still not much," Owen said.

"I'm glad kids don't work like that today," I said.

"It took a long time to enact the laws that eventually stopped child labor," noted Professor Tuesday. "In 1938 Congress took action and passed what was called the Fair Labor Standards Act. This law stopped companies from hiring young children for dangerous work."

"There's one other thing she told me," I added. "Sophia said that she quit school after the third grade."

"No way," replied Owen.

"Way," answered the professor. "Back then children often left school once they learned to read, write, and do some simple math."

"What kind of work did Sophia's mother do?" Owen asked.

"She didn't say," Rachel answered.

"While children in the family worked, Polish mothers usually stayed at home," said the professor. "Some women who did work outside of the home had unusual jobs."

"Like what?"

The professor smiled, "One of the jobs Polish women did in the Detroit area was to make cigars."

"Cigars?" Owen asked as he made a funny face. "Like the stinky cigars my grandpa used to smoke?"

"That's right," said the professor, "many women had jobs rolling cigars in factories."

"I wouldn't do that job," I said. "Oh, one more thing—Sophia also told me that she had to walk a long way to and from her work."

"That was often the case," the professor added. "We visited her in a time that was well before the invention of the automobile. Some traveled by horse and buggy, but for many people, walking was the only way to get to work or to market."

"What did the three of you do while Rachel and I were talking to Sophia?" I asked.

Owen got very excited. "We took a long walk across the field and saw a factory." Owen covered a smile as he continued, "Of course we watched where we were walking because we knew that cows grazed in that field."

"What did they make in the factory?" Rachel asked.

"I'm not sure," said Owen. "They were making big box-like things—so big you could walk around in them."

"They were making railroad cars," said the professor. "Railroads, like the Erie Canal, helped millions of immigrants come to and settle in Michigan. They also provided an easy and economical way to move goods around the state."

"What was the factory like?" I asked.

"It was dirty and dusty, dark and noisy, too. It didn't look like a very good place to work," Owen said. "My dad works in a factory, and he has to wear a safety helmet and safety glasses all the time. None of those guys in that factory had a helmet or anything else."

"It seems like all kinds of work was dirty, dusty, and dangerous in those days," Rachel added.

"They didn't have most of the safety equipment we use today," said the professor as he adjusted his glasses up and down. "Many workers, including children, were hurt on the job. At this particular factory, they were making wooden railroad cars. In just a few years the company would be changing to make railroad cars out of steel so heavier loads could be carried."

An Immigrant Visit
The Professor's Office—Today

When we finished our talk and our snacks, we heard a knock at the professor's door.

"Who is it?" the professor called out.

"It is me, Professor," a voice called back from the other side of the door.

"Come in, come in," said the professor. "Let me introduce you to my friends." A tall dark-skinned student walked into the room. He was very slender. His hair was cut short, and his face wore a big, bright smile. The professor turned to Owen and me. "This is Jesse, Rachel, and Owen. Of course you have already met my nephew, Mister Adams."

"I am pleased to meet you," the young man said. "My name is Yak."

His voice and smile were very friendly. The way he spoke was interesting to me. It is hard to describe, but it was like he bit off each word as he talked.

"Are you visiting Professor Tuesday as I am?" Yak said.

"Yes, we are," said Owen. "Rachel and I are working on a special assignment for school. Our friend, Jesse, came with us. The professor is helping us learn about immigration in Michigan."

"That is a wonderful topic," Yak said, "for I am an immigrant to your state."

"Where did you migrate from?" I asked.

"I came here with my mother and my brothers from the Republic of Sudan," Yak said. "Do you know where that is?"

Owen and I shook our heads no. Mister Adams walked over to a map and pointed to a spot in the northeast of the continent of Africa.

"Yes, Mister Adams, it is in Africa. It is the largest of all the countries in Africa," Yak said. "Most people there speak either Arabic or English."

"Tell them why you left Sudan, Yak," said the professor.

"There was a terrible war where my family lived," Yak said. His face was suddenly sad. "My father went off to war and I have not seen or heard from him for many years. War is very terrible. We had no food, our houses and villages were destroyed, and there was no medicine for the sick. We ran away to save ourselves."

"Africa is far, far away," Owen said. "How did you come to Michigan?"

"People from a church rescued my family," Yak said. "They helped us to escape from Sudan. They have also helped us get a house and a job for our mother. My brothers and I now go to school."

As we talked with Yak, Rachel was writing notes as fast as she could.

"Where does your mother work?" Owen asked.

Yak smiled. "My mother works at a hospital."

"Is she a doctor or a nurse?" I asked.

"No," Yak replied. "She cleans at the hospital. You know, she scrubs floors and makes beds. It is very hard work and she does not make much money, but she is happy to have a job. She is also very pleased that we are doing well in school. I work hard to make her proud."

Mister Adams signed a message to Professor Tuesday. When he was finished, the professor nodded his head. "I'll ask Yak."

The professor turned to Yak, "Mister Adams wants to know what the differences are between Michigan and the Republic of Sudan."

Yak laughed out loud, "Everything is different. There is no war. The people have been very kind here in Michigan. The food is different—it is very good and there is lots of it compared to the Sudan. In the north of Sudan is a large desert. It is very hot in most of the country. In Michigan it can be very cold. I do not like the cold."

"My friend Yak is a perfect example of immigrants who are still coming to Michigan," said the professor. "All the settlements and towns we have visited have seen many new immigrants. People think of the town of Hamtramck as Poletown ... or a Polish community. But, even the community of Hamtramck is being changed. Immigrants from places like Yemen and Bangladesh have moved to the city.

The professor thought for a moment before he continued. "Today, Michigan is home to a large Arab-American population. Other recent immigrants include people from India, China, Mexico, Canada, Eastern Europe, Laos, Germany, Thailand, Korea, the United Kingdom, and Poland. Long ago many people came to Michigan through the seaport of Detroit. Today, they come through a different port ... the airport. Detroit Metropolitan Airport is one of the busiest airports in the world."

The professor returned to his laptop and did a search. "Ah, here it is," he said. "A recent study indicates that just over 8 percent of Michigan's population does not speak English at home. That's very interesting."

"Does that mean some immigrants don't learn English?" Rachel asked.

"For some people, learning a new language is very difficult," noted the professor. "Young people usually have an easier time of it."

"That is true with my mother," Yak said. "My brothers and I learned to speak English very quickly. It is harder for her. Many people have a hard time understanding her when she talks."

"Some immigrant groups wanted to learn the English language so they would be thought of as Americans rather than foreigners," added the professor. "Others preferred to keep the culture of their former countries, so they are less interested in learning a different language."

"Think about Frankenmuth and Holland, Michigan," said the professor. "Though many different people have moved to those cities, each town works hard to keep their German and Dutch heritages alive. These towns and others across the state celebrate their ethnic pride with wonderful restaurants, festivals, and celebrations."

"My father took me to a Greektown festival in Detroit," Rachel said. "It was fun! The food there was the best I've ever had."

"Ah, yes," replied Professor Tuesday, "the area in and around Detroit is very diverse. Several cultures celebrate their uniqueness. You mentioned Greektown. There's also Corktown, which is largely Irish. Mexicantown is a proud ethnic community in Detroit. And, as we have seen, Hamtramck still maintains much of its Polish heritage."

"What about African Americans?" I asked.

"Unfortunately, we haven't had time today to study the immigration of black people to Michigan. Several famous African Americans call Michigan their home," replied the professor as he tapped a pencil on his desk. "Many came from the south to Michigan to find work, especially work in the automotive industry. During the awful time of slavery in our country, Michigan was a famous stop on the Underground Railroad—a road to freedom for many, many slaves."

"Can we take just one more trip back in time to learn more about black immigrants?" I asked. "Please?"

"I'm sorry," said the professor. "I have some important work to finish before the end of the day, so our time is over even though there are many places and times that would be wonderful to visit. If you or your classmates would like to learn more about African Americans in Michigan, I would be happy to help you another day."

Professor Tuesday stood up. "I must get back to work now. Tuesday is almost over and Tuesdays are important to me, you know."

"Thank you for all your help, Professor," Owen said as he shook the professor's hand.

"Yes, thank you very much," Rachel added.

When I added my thanks, Mister Adams ran across the room to us. He hugged Owen, Rachel, and then me. Then the professor's nephew stuck out his hand to shake ours.

"It was a pleasure meeting you," said Mister Adams in a loud, booming voice.

Our mouths hung open. "Mister Adams! You just talked," I said.

"Of course I did," replied Mister Adams.

"Why haven't you said anything before?" asked the professor.

"I didn't have anything to say," answered Mister Adams.

The Report

Arrowhead School— The Following Monday

Owen and Rachel went to work on their report on the Sunday after our visit with Professor Tuesday. Owen's mother dropped him off at Rachel's house. They took seats at the kitchen table and started.

"I've got an idea," Rachel said. "Why don't we trade journals? That way you can see what I wrote, and I can see what you wrote."

"Okay," said Owen. He handed Rachel his journal and she slid hers across the table to him.

Rachel was shocked when she opened Owen's journal. "You didn't write very much."

"So what?" Owen replied. "I wrote some notes and drew some pictures. You wrote a lot of junk that we probably won't even use."

"This will never do," Rachel said angrily. "I want a good grade on this report, and you aren't helping."

Rachel and Owen started arguing, just like they did in Miss Pepper's class. Then Owen held up his hand. The room went quiet for a moment.

"Wait," he said, "I've got a great idea."

"Yah, right," Rachel replied. "So, what's this great idea?"

"You are good at writing, I am good at drawing," he said. "Why don't we use your words and my pictures to make the report? If we work together, it could make a great project."

"That's not a bad idea," Rachel said, "not a bad idea at all."

"It's sort of like the immigrants of Michigan," Owen added. "They were different, but they had to work together to make a great state."

The two of them worked through the afternoon, sharing ideas and points they wanted to include in their report. Owen scanned some of his pictures and created a presentation on the computer. That way they could show the report to the whole class all at once. Rachel's mother checked in on them from time to time. They showed her their report as they worked on it. She was very excited and thought the two of them did a great job.

Owen, Rachel, and I walked to school together the next day. They were both pleased about their report. When we entered Miss Pepper's classroom, we had the shock of our lives. There, talking with

Miss Pepper, was a lady who looked strangely like the professor. Mister Adams and Professor Tuesday sat next to her. The professor's nephew ran up and gave us big hugs.

The lady sitting next to Professor Tuesday had bright red hair and freckles. She wore big glasses like the professor and even shrugged her shoulders like he did.

"You must be Mrs. Sweetie Pie," Rachel said. "I am pleased to meet you. I'm sure you must have heard this before, but Mister Adams is a great kid."

Sweetie Pie said, "Thank you, I am very proud of him. He does wander off now and then, though."

"We know," Owen said as he rolled his eyes. "So, what are you all doing here?"

"We're here to see your report. I wouldn't miss it for the world," said Professor Tuesday.

"Me either," said Mister Adams. "We are very eager to hear what you have to say."

"Okay," Rachel said, "but you can't wander off during our presentation, Mister Adams."

We all had a good laugh. When the bell rang, Owen and Rachel took their seats. Professor Tuesday, Sweetie Pie, and Mister Adams sat in the back of the room. After the Pledge of Allegiance and morning announcements, Miss Pepper walked to the front of the classroom.

"Today, we have a special report by Rachel and Owen," our teacher announced. "And, we also have special guests with us." Miss Pepper pointed to the back of the room. "Many of you will remember

Professor Tuesday. The young man with him is the professor's nephew, Mister Adams, and the professor's sister, Mrs. Sweetie Pie."

Some of the kids in the class started laughing, but Rachel stopped them. "That's enough of that," she said. "Maybe Mister Adams and Mrs. Sweetie Pie have unusual names, but that's no reason to laugh at them. All of us have to be more understanding of others."

Robert, the class troublemaker, spoke up, "Is that you, Rachel, or did some alien take over your body?"

Rachel stared at him. "Maybe I've changed, Robert. Maybe I have realized that nobody's perfect ... not even you."

Robert shut his big trap and sat back in his seat. Owen went to set up the computer and the projector while Rachel took their report to the front of the classroom.

When everything was ready, Rachel began. "This is a report on immigrants to Michigan. It was prepared by Owen and me with the help of Professor Tuesday and Mister Adams ... Oh, and Jesse, too."

Owen started the presentation with a picture he had drawn of the Erie Canal, and Rachel talked about everything we learned during our visit. Then it was Owen's turn as he told everyone about frontier Detroit. Owen joked about how he was sneezing and tripping all the time. He even showed his muddy sneaker to the class. Everybody laughed.

The report they'd written together shared the story of many of the immigrants to Michigan, but they were careful to tell everyone that there were many more immigrants to our state that they couldn't talk about because they didn't have the time.

After the presentation the class was very quiet. You could hear a pin drop. Suddenly Professor Tuesday, Mister Adams, and Mrs. Sweetie Pie stood up and clapped loudly. Then the whole class and Miss Pepper stood and clapped with them. It was very exciting.

When the room settled down, some of our classmates had questions.

"What was the coolest thing you saw?" Nathan asked.

"All the ships in frontier Detroit," answered Owen, "and the big fish on Mackinac Island were cool, too."

"I don't know if it was the coolest thing I saw," Rachel said, "but talking with the Polish girl in Hamtramck was fun and interesting."

Miss Pepper raised her hand and Rachel called on her. "What was the most important thing you learned?"

"It may sound silly," she said, "but Owen and I never used to get along. Everyone knows we argued all the time. So, the most important thing I learned is that we all need to get along with each other. Immigrants had to do it. That was the only way they could survive."

"That is a very good answer," said Miss Pepper. "I think you both deserve an *A* on your report."

I was very proud of my friends.

Before Rachel and Owen took their seats, Tamika asked one final question. "If you could go back in history one more time, what would you like to see?"

"I would like to learn more about the Underground Railroad and African-American people in our state," Rachel answered. "And, Professor Tuesday told Owen and me that he would be interested in helping us learn more."

Professor Tuesday smiled, nodding his head in approval. Mister Adams made the "okay" sign.

THE END

Author's Notebook

1. **Family History**—What is your family history? Can you trace your family back to a foreign nation or a different part of the United States? Interview family members and relatives to learn about your personal history. Consider writing a paper about how your family came to Michigan.

2. **Conflict**—Owen and Rachel just can't get along. Their constant arguing is an important part of the story. Writers often use conflict to keep the reader's interest and teach lessons about cooperation. How do Rachel and Owen overcome their differences and learn to get along?

3. **American Sign Language**—Throughout most of the story, Mister Adams communicates in sign language. Many schools teach the American Sign Language alphabet and common phrases. You can learn more about sign language at www.lifeprint.com.

4. **Character Development**—Owen, Rachel, Jesse, Mister Adams, and Professor Tuesday are five completely different people. Authors try to create unique characters when writing stories. Write a short description of each character in your own words.

5. **Immigrant Destinations**—Immigrants have moved and continue to move to cities around the state of Michigan. Local museums and libraries often have information about the immigrants who have come to your area. Consider a field trip to learn more about the immigrants who have settled in your community.

6. **Voice**—Part of story writing is to create a different "sounding" voice for each character in the story. Creating a voice that the reader can't actually hear is both fun and challenging. Try to write some things that Rachel would say to Owen. Then use a different "voice" to write Owen's response.

7. **Fun**—Whether it's an amusement park or a good joke, people love to have fun. During this story, each character has an opportunity to enjoy some fun. What was your favorite moment? Write a story about something funny that happened to you.

8. **Fear**—Scary moments help to make a story fun to read. The author has included several scary moments in this story. Which one did you enjoy the most? Consider writing a ghost story about an immigrant relative who comes alive to tell you about your past.

9. **Symbolism**—In this story the professor's computer has a problem, and Owen finds that it has a conflict in the software. This situation is symbolic of the conflict between Owen and Rachel. Make a list of things that may represent similarities between a computer conflict and a human conflict.

10. **Mister Adams**—The professor's nephew, Mister Adams, is an interesting character. What things about Mister Adams did you find interesting or funny? Mister Adams is named after the second President of the United States, John Adams. Are you named after someone? Do you know anyone else who may be named after a family member or a famous person? Consider writing a report about President John Adams ... he is one of the author's favorite presidents, too.